LEAGUE OF STRAYS

LEAGUE OF STRAYS

L. B. SCHULMAN

AMULET BOOKS | NEW YORK

Library of Congress Cataloging-in-Publication Data

Schulman, L. B.
League of Strays / by L. B. Schulman.
p. cm.
Summary: An alluring, manipulative student convinces a group of social misfits to come together for friendship and to get back at the classmates and teachers who have wronged them.
ISBN 978-1-4197-0403-1 (alk. paper)
[1. Friendship—Fiction. 2. Revenge—Fiction. 3. Loyalty—Fiction. 4. High schools—Fiction. 5. Schools—Fiction.] I. Title.
PZ7.S38664Le 2012
[E]—dc23
2012008315

Amulet Books are available at special discounts when purchased in quantity for premiums and promotions as well as fundraising or educational use. Special editions can also be created to specification. For details, contact specialsales@abramsbooks.com or the address below.

THE ART OF BOOKS SINCE 1949
115 West 18th Street
New York, NY 10011
www.abramsbooks.com

FOR MY FAMILY

♪ CHAPTER 1 ♪

I PEDALED DOWN THE SIDE OF THE ROAD, RELYING ON passing headlights to lead my way. No one knew I was out here. No one. What if a car slammed into me, knocking me into a ditch? If I didn't die from my injuries, I'd freeze to death long before anyone spotted my crumpled bike.

A bitter January gust whipped my hair into my eyes. I was shivering so hard, I could barely steer my bike in a straight line. I pulled my hood up with one shaking hand while cars honked and swerved, choking me with their exhaust fumes.

I veered onto the dirt and climbed off my bike, coughing so hard that it brought tears to my eyes. This was the craziest thing I'd ever done, and right now it didn't seem worth it. As I waited for a caravan of trucks to rumble by, I dried my sweaty palms on my jeans, crinkling the paper inside my pocket to make sure that the letter I'd found in the mailbox—without a stamp or return address—was still there. What kind of meeting required sneaking out of the house at ten on a school night, anyway? But I knew if I didn't show up, I'd never find out.

My worst fear was that this was all some kind of joke. If it was, I knew who was behind it. I'd been Tiffany Miller's scapegoat since kindergarten, and it had only gotten worse in middle school. She used to stick gum in my hair, and when I wore something new, she left her mark with a pen. Kid stuff, Mom had said. Whatever, it still stung.

Five months ago, right before my senior year, the Law Offices of Posner and Huggins had offered my father a partnership. Moving won't be so bad, I'd thought, other than leaving my best friend, Sofie. It was only to a different part of the state. But the laugh was on me when Tiffany's father, a corporal in the Army, transferred his family to the military base a few miles away. How nice, Mom had said, a familiar face at your new school. But then, she'd always been out of touch with reality. Mine, at least.

The thing was, the invitation wasn't really Tiffany's style. She wasn't the type to plan ahead. What if someone else wrote the letter, someone who really did want me to join a special club? Yeah, right, I told myself, trying to keep my expectations in check. Since starting school, no one had asked me anything deeper than "What's your name?" or "Where'd you come from?" But at five foot ten, with a mass of curls that went through a bottle of Frizz-Ease every month, I didn't exactly blend in with the cement-block walls. What if someone had noticed me?

I finally reached Stafford Pond and leaned my bike against a cracked bench dotted with bird crap. My stomach contracted as I turned around in a circle, careful not to leave my back exposed for more than a second. Was someone hiding out there, watching me?

Nothing.

I scanned the opaque curtain of trees, searching for the whites of an eye, the flash of a camera, the sound of hushed laughter. I'd prepared myself for many scenarios, but not *nothing.* My pulse throbbed in my ears, muffling the rattle of the wind through the trees. I checked the time on my cell phone. Eight minutes after ten. What if they'd thought I wasn't going to show up and had already left?

I exhaled slowly to calm my heart, which was still thrashing inside me from the stress of sneaking out of my house. The sliding glass door had offered the perfect escape route. Of course, I'd only made it halfway up the hilly side yard before I slipped on a patch of ice and went flying into a rusted wheelbarrow that pitched to the side with a dramatic *thwack.* I'd crawled behind the air-conditioner unit and peered around it into the living room.

Mom had been stretched out on the couch, a leg on Dad's lap. She'd eyed the window before turning back to her favorite weight-loss show. They probably couldn't imagine that their daughter would be anywhere except in bed. The trust I'd "earned" over the years was proof of my boring life.

Only, tonight wasn't so boring. I was standing in the middle of a desolate park like a bull's-eye. I glanced at the massive mulberry tree that stood guard over the pond. If I climbed it, I could see *them* before they saw *me.* I reached for the lowest branch and hauled myself up. I hadn't been in a tree since I was a kid, and this was the second one in a night—the first having been the escape route outside my raised bedroom porch. *Very mature, Charlotte, playing in trees. I'm sure whoever's watching is real impressed.* I tried not to think about the possibility that I'd just trapped myself up here.

The full moon beamed a spotlight on the icy surface of the pond. Everything was still. *Too* still. I worked to free the letter from my pocket, careful not to lose my grip and plummet to the ground.

Ironing the invitation with a fist, I read it for what must've been the hundredth time:

Dear Charlotte,

You have been chosen to join the League of Strays. A secret meeting will be held at Stafford Pond, fourth picnic table on the right at 10:00, Wednesday night. Come alone. Make sure nobody follows you, or you won't hear from us again.

—K.

I squinted at the signature. Was it a K or a cursive T? Even Tiffany wouldn't be stupid enough to sign her own initial. Besides, it definitely looked like a K.

I twisted around at a noise and lost my footing. I managed to hook an arm on a branch, saving myself from a broken bone or two. What the hell was I doing out in the woods at night?

And that's when I saw Nora Walker, genius extraordinaire, emerge from the dark. She walked straight to the picnic table and sat down, head swiveling like a security camera in a bank. My heart plunged to the ground like a kite with a hole in it.

Nora didn't qualify as the secret-admirer type. In fact, I couldn't think of a single reason she would ask me to meet her here. But since I'd come all this way, I owed it to myself to find out.

I slid down the tree, the bark cutting into my arm. Nora jumped three inches. "Dammit, who's there?"

"Charlotte Brody." I took a hesitant step forward.

Her arms and legs crossed in perfect synchronization. "Why'd you send me this note?"

I stared at her, bewildered. "I didn't," I said, waving my letter at her. "I got one, too." I hesitated for a moment, then asked, "Do you know a girl named Tiffany Miller?"

"Who?"

"Never mind."

Nora gestured for me to take the seat beside her. I walked around the table and sat down on the opposite side.

"If no one comes in two minutes, I'm leaving." She nudged her silver-rimmed glasses up the bridge of her nose. "I have a paper due in AP biology on the caliber of fetal versus adult stem cells in disease management." Whenever Nora opened her mouth, it sounded like she was reciting from the vocabulary section of an SAT prep book.

My favorite theory, the one where I'd been selected to join an elite organization, disintegrated like a wet paper towel now that she was here. We were too different to belong to the same club. But Nora wanted to see what this was all about, just like me.

I spun around at the sound of crunching leaves. Zoe Carpenter, dressed in her usual oversized army jacket, tight black jeans, and trashed hiking boots, glared at us. "Take it you guys are joining the big bad League, too?" She rotated the flashlight in her hand, aiming the light under her chin. "Spooky place for a rendezvous, huh?"

Zoe scared me, the way she stomped through the halls like a military officer trying to put the fear of God in her underlings. She practically lived inside that shapeless camouflage jacket. But now that she was close, I was surprised to see that she was pretty. Her eyes looked like green beach glass against a coffee-with-cream complexion. Too bad about her personality, though.

Nora made a show of rolling her eyes. "Oh, please. I just want to see who sent the note."

Before I could digest the effect of Zoe's arrival on my ever-changing theories, a bush rustled nearby. My heart slammed against my chest. Our heads whipped around in unison, waiting for whatever lurked inside to announce itself.

It turned out to be a tall guy in a leather jacket and faded blue jeans a shade darker than his pale eyes, which were fringed with the kind of lashes most girls would kill for. The moonlight bounced off his glossy black hair.

It seemed that Nora and Zoe weren't immune to his good looks, either. Nora's eyes widened behind her owl glasses, and Zoe stopped chomping on the wad of gum in her mouth. The pink blob, stuck on the tip of her tongue, dropped to the ground.

"Hello, everyone. I'm Kade Harlin, and I'd like to officially welcome you to the League of Strays." His voice was as deep and resonant as the bassoon in our school orchestra.

Kade Harlin. I repeated the name under my breath, letting the rhythm of it roll off my tongue.

"Nice hairdo," Zoe quipped. I couldn't tell if she was complimenting or insulting the shiny peaks that jutted from his head in random directions. I decided it wasn't a case of accidental bed head. Advanced gel construction all the way. I wished I could touch them. Did they feel like feathers or cactus spines?

Kade smiled, flashing even, white teeth. I found myself smiling back, late at night, at a guy I'd never seen before in my life.

He gestured behind him. "This is my friend Richie." I focused on the small shadow and cringed. Mom and Dad would freak out if they knew their precious daughter was standing a few feet away from the school drug dealer.

"And that makes all five of us," Kade finished.

The more I studied him, the more I determined the geometric spikes were a work of art. I peeled my eyes off his carefully crafted hair to scan the woods one last time. Thankfully, Tiffany Miller wasn't behind a tree, giggling into the arm of her Abercrombie & Fitch scoop-neck cardigan.

"You want to tell us what's going on?" Nora barked.

"I intend to," Kade said, sitting on top of the picnic table. I moved over to make room for his long legs. "You've each been selected to join the League of Strays. We've been profiling you for months."

Profiling? Wasn't that how the FBI identified potential terrorists in airports? A chill rippled up the back of my neck.

"It's not a club," he said. "It's a selective group of friends."

I suppressed a smile. A selective group comprised of a bunch of social misfits? I realized I was including myself in that definition. But I wasn't a misfit. Not really. Maybe I hadn't won any popularity contests at my old school, but I'd had friends at least.

On the other hand, I didn't have any right now. Sure, I had people to say hi to at orchestra practice. But no one to meet between classes or hang out with after school.

Zoe dropped a hand on her hip. "You're full of it, Kade."

"Zoe Carpenter. Let's see, mom divorced Zoe's stepfather last year. Well, technically, he was number three." His voice was warm and easy, without a hint of condescension. "She lives in a home of revolving men, but the only one her mom really loves is Jack . . . Daniel's."

Zoe catapulted from the bench. "You don't know shit about my mother. Or me." She stalked away, crushing the leaves and twigs under her boots.

"Nora Walker," Kade continued, unfazed. Zoe froze, then craned her head to hear him. "Mom and dad work seventy-hour weeks at their high-tech jobs. Needless to say, they aren't around much. When she was twelve, Nora's fifteen-year-old sister committed suicide by downing all of her mother's migraine medicine. Now an only child, Nora makes it her personal mission to erase her parents' pain."

I didn't have siblings myself, but I could imagine what it would feel like to have a sister kill herself. No wonder Nora was so obsessed with her grades. She must be doing everything in her power to make her family happy.

"Perfection takes a lot of energy," Kade added.

I half expected Nora to take a stab at Kade's face before exiting stage right, but she just propped a fist under her chin. "Pretty thorough, Harlin."

"There's one thing I can promise," Kade said. "I'll be honest with all of you, which is more than I can say for most people."

I glanced at Zoe. Her mouth tightened as she looked at the trees hunching forward in the breeze. I expected her to challenge his definition of the truth, especially as it applied to her own life, but she didn't.

Kade turned to me with a smile that could melt an Alaskan glacier. "Charlotte Brody."

I studied my black Keds with sudden interest. At least he couldn't have much on me. Not with my dull life.

He unfurled his arms like he was presenting me at a debutante ball or something. "The new kid in town."

Nora laughed. I started to smile but hung my head to hide it. I imagined Kade following me from class to class, taking notes. The idea of someone spying on me was definitely creepy. Even so, I wanted to hear more. What else did Kade Harlin think about me?

"Charlotte's a good judge of character, which explains why she can't find real friends at Kennedy High," he said. "She lives in a bubble, her every move dictated by Mommy and Daddy. She's applied to the Barrymore School of Music to study the viola, but it's really their dream, not hers."

Coming to Kennedy High at the start of senior year had been a lot harder than I'd expected. When I was younger, everyone wanted to get to know the new kid. But in high school, it seemed like people were happy with, or at least tolerant of, whatever friendships they already had. Not to mention that making friends took effort, and really, who had time for that when there were college applications, never-ending homework, and boyfriend dramas to deal with.

I stared at him, speechless. How did he know about Barrymore? I hadn't told a soul, other than my music teachers and the college-placement counselor. And he thought it was *my parents'* dream, not mine? I'd played the viola since the third grade and was now first chair in the school orchestra. You didn't get that far without a serious dedication to music. In fact, Mr. Watson, my private teacher, said my audition CD for the most prestigious music college in the Midwest was "undeniable," and he couldn't understand why I'd bothered applying to State as a backup.

I stayed quiet, though, not wanting to look defensive. Kade might think he knew all about me, but on this count, he was dead wrong.

"She hasn't found anything better to do," he said. "But that's about to change."

My insides flopped like a fish washed up on the beach. What was going to change? And *how?*

In three giant steps, he reached Zoe, who still had her back to him. He laid a hand on her shoulder. She recoiled from his touch. "Being alone sucks, but you don't have to live like this anymore," he said softly.

Was Zoe lonely? It didn't seem like it when you saw her barreling down the hallway, hollering at people to get out of her way. Then again, it was easier to reject people before they had a chance to reject you.

Zoe shot him a nasty look. "Why us, Kade? I'm sure there are a lot of people who'd like to be your friend. Why, out of all the wonderful choices out there, did you pick us?"

When he didn't give an answer, she asked, "So what about you and your pal? Don't we get to hear all about your personal issues?"

Kade looked thoughtful, as if she'd asked him something major. "Richie and I went to another school before we switched to Kennedy High in the tenth grade. We've gone through a lot, but our friendship's stronger because of it."

They changed schools *together*? I wanted to know more, but instead of telling us, Kade flipped his palms up as if asking the good Lord to bless us. "The League is a gathering of people who need each other. It's instant friendship. We won't have to watch our backs anymore. We're here to support and protect each other." Kade's gaze stopped on me, and I followed the tip of his tongue as it traced the curve of his upper lip.

Beside him, Zoe made a subtle gagging motion, mocking his words. Nora tried to hide a smile but lost. The exchange lasted five seconds tops, but Kade caught it. He looked disappointed, like they just didn't get it. I felt an overwhelming urge to tell them to shut up and listen to what he had to say.

"Protect each other from what? I have friends," Nora murmured.

"Would they put out their necks to save you?" he asked.

Kade Harlin was acting like we were lifelong friends instead of a bunch of strangers shivering together in the woods on a January night. I wondered what he knew that I didn't.

"Friends are overrated," Zoe said, returning to the picnic table. She pulled a boot up onto the bench and dropped her chin onto her knee. Nora scowled at Zoe's shoes and shifted to the edge until she almost fell off.

"Or maybe it's hard to get close to them when your home life's a wreck," he said. "Listen, it doesn't matter where we come from. If we can open ourselves to the possibilities of the League, nothing can stop us." He paused, meeting each of our eyes in turn. "And besides, there's strength in numbers."

He glanced again in my direction, then turned and walked away. Richie scrambled to keep up with him. I almost expected a puff of wind to blow in, dispersing them like dandelion seeds.

Zoe waited until Kade had faded into the backdrop of the trees. "Disturbing," she said.

"Bizarre," Nora added.

"Totally," I said.

The three of us looked around, avoiding each other's eyes. I wished they'd say something to summarize what had just happened. Finally, I mumbled good-bye, hopped on my bike, and left them sitting on the bench.

♪ CHAPTER 2 ♪

THE NEXT MORNING, I SHUFFLED LIKE A ZOMBIE INTO THE dining room. I had been up until two in the morning, replaying in my head all the things Kade had said about the League.

I hitched my backpack onto my shoulder and headed for the door. "See you later, Mom," I said.

She poked her head out of the kitchen pass-through and wagged a wooden spoon at me. "Not without breakfast."

Turning one's back on a nutritional opportunity was a major offense in my mother's manual. God help me if I didn't finish every last carrot in my lunch, or if I made a snack within an hour of dinner. Some of Mom's rules were completely unreasonable. Like me not drinking coffee, for example. She thinks it's danger-ous. You know, accelerated heart rates, energy fluctuations, the addictive nature of caffeine, and so on.

She swooped into the dining room with a bowl of oatmeal,

a glass of orange juice, and buttered toast divided into four symmetrical triangles. I devoured it in a record time of one minute and eighteen seconds, then tried to make an escape.

"Charlotte?" she called after me.

I glanced over my shoulder. "Yeah?"

"You forgot to take your vitamin today."

"Mom, I'm late . . ."

She rushed from the room. I waited. It wasn't easy being an only child, scrutinized like a sample on a slide. Mom returned with a massive vitamin displayed on an outstretched palm.

I considered what Kade had said: *Charlotte lives in a bubble, her every move dictated by Mommy and Daddy.* I reached for the vitamin, then chugged it down with a glass of O.J., wondering if maybe he had a point.

"You look nice today," Mom said. "I like the eye shadow."

The lure of the League and seeing Kade at school had coaxed its way into what little sleep I'd had. My dreams had been disjointed, but I knew he'd been in them. When I woke up, I'd dug through the cabinet under the sink to search for the Sephora makeup kit I got for Hanukkah two years ago. Safety seal intact.

"You don't like to wear makeup," Mom said, fishing for details.

I figured there wasn't much I could do about my boyish body and frizzy brown ringlets. The face was all I had. I just hoped someone besides my mother would notice.

"Well, there's a first for everything," I said, bolting for the door.

On the front steps, I pulled out a compact. The blush "livened up winter skin," just like the back of the box had promised. The rose-colored lip gloss did a decent job masking my chapped lips. But my face felt sticky, which is why I never wore the stuff. Still, it was hard to argue with the improvement.

I batted my eyes in the mirror, practicing for who-knows-what. When I stopped flirting with myself long enough to take another look, I groaned. Oh God. Flecks of mascara, everywhere. I tried to erase them with my pinkie and ended up creating two black eyes. So much for the new-and-improved me.

"You forgot something," Mom called, her head out the window.

I glanced down at my empty hand. How could I forget my viola? I never forgot my viola. It was practically an appendage.

"You're going to be late, Charlotte!" Mom said as I ran back in, scooped up my instrument, and darted outside again. I hopped over the yellow recycle bin on the sidewalk and kept going.

At the intersection, I checked to make sure Mr. Hanford wasn't watching before cutting through his backyard. The Kennedy High parking lot was packed, as always. A few kids sprawled on the hoods of secondhand cars they'd bought with summer-job money, talking on cell phones—probably to each other. The warning bell rang but no one moved.

I raced toward the three buildings joined by glass-encased hallways and veered right to Building C, where most of the senior classes were held. Inside the double doors, a mass of bodies sucked me into its fold. I searched through the crowd for a certain spiky hairstyle.

"Keep moving," a guy said, knocking me into a girl who was checking her lipstick in the reflective side of her sunglasses. She gave me a caustic look.

"I'm sorry," I said.

No problem, Charlotte, I wanted her to say. It would be nice if someone actually knew my name.

"Whatever," she said, shutting her locker door.

By third period, I was officially frustrated. Where the heck was Kade? The League of Strays wasn't much of a friendship group without him. Hoping for a sighting, I took the long way to class—up the stairs to the second-floor hallway and back down the other end. I got a late mark in calculus for my efforts.

Fifty minutes later, I slipped into the girls' restroom and scrubbed my face with school-issue brown paper towels. I guess when you try too hard, nothing happens. Now that the no-fuss Charlotte was back, I convinced myself that Kade would be waiting for me when I came out, leaning against the wall, one leg bent behind him. The image in my head was so clear that when I walked out and he wasn't there, I felt stood up.

In orchestra, the noise, usually off the charts, buzzed at a low level. I took my viola out of its case and wound my way through the semicircle of seats. I liked to get in a few minutes of practice before class started.

I was tuning my strings when Amie Newman, my stand partner, came up behind me. "Did you hear about Mrs. Tutti?"

I shook my head. "Where is she?"

Amie's face creased with concern. "Nervous breakdown.

I heard she's in solitary confinement at a mental ward some-where."

"Wow." It was all I could get out.

Three months earlier, Mrs. Tutti's husband died from an aneurism. He was only fifty-one. She took a few weeks off, but when she came back, she seemed almost normal. I hadn't said anything to her. What could I say that wouldn't sound lame? Now I wondered if maybe I hadn't searched for the words hard enough.

"She was my favorite teacher," I said, wincing at my choice of verb tense. "*Is*, I mean."

Kids complained that Mrs. Tutti pushed too hard, mostly because she demanded short nails and daily practice logs. She was tough, but that's why our orchestra had placed first at nationals. Mrs. Tutti was the kind of teacher who cared about more than a paycheck. Like when budget cuts forced one of the school counselors to go part-time and she signed on as a volunteer assistant counselor.

Amie looked like she was about to add something when a woman with tortoiseshell glasses weaved through the violin section toward the conductor stand.

"Hello, everyone. My name is Maddy Irving, and I'll be your substitute. As you may have heard, your teacher is out on sick leave. For now, please team up with your stand partner and prac-tice the"—she glanced at her notepad—"Mussorgsky?"

Mrs. Irving forgot to take roll until the dismissal bell rang, making me late for lunch. Up until November, I'd been able to sit outside and eat my bag lunch under the sprawling sycamore tree in front of the school theater. The weather had forced me back inside. I'd taken to spending my lunch period in the orchestra practice room, where I wolfed down my pastrami sandwich and got a decent half hour of practice in.

This time, though, I headed for the cafeteria, a place I normally avoided at all costs. It wasn't designed to hold all of us at once. We fit in, the way you can always get an extra shirt into a piece of luggage, but it wasn't pleasant.

Kids scurried around me like a colony of ants. I searched for Kade and his drug-dealing sidekick; for Nora, her nose in a textbook; for Zoe, pretending she could nap while waiting in the lunch line. I couldn't find any of them. I sighed, scanning the room until I spotted one mostly empty table. I headed for it, passing Tiffany Miller, surrounded by her loyal subjects, trading lipsticks and giggling.

By the time I reached the table, there was only one seat left. A force slammed into my shoulder, pushing me to the side. A girl bulldozed past and slid into my chair. She examined the contents of her bag lunch to avoid my scathing glare.

Lunch at Kennedy was like musical chairs, only without the music or the fun.

Three tables over, a guy rose to his feet, lunch tray topping the sci-fi books in his arms. I dropped into his vacated seat. As I pulled the carrots from my bag, I heard a scraping noise behind me. Zoe, scooting her chair my way. She didn't say hello, just flipped open a book and started to read. I glanced at the title and laughed out loud. *How to Win Friends and Influence People*, by Dale

Carnegie. Her hair fell like a curtain around her face, parting just enough for me to see the corners of her mouth lift up.

"Rule number one: take an interest in other people," she said, slapping the book shut. "So where the hell is he?"

"Who?" I asked stupidly.

"I bet he blew off school. Do you think this was a joke? If it was, I'll kick his ass, swear to God."

I lifted the corner of my whole wheat bread and nudged the lettuce back from the edge. *No, of course it wasn't a joke,* I wanted to say. *How could it be? That would be too mean.* But I didn't say anything.

"I guess that League stuff was all a bunch of crap, huh? I was buying it, too," Zoe said.

"The whole thing feels surreal, like it didn't even happen," I added.

We sat there, wondering, as we ate our lunches. Zoe had a Key lime pie yogurt and a Mountain Dew. That was it.

I decided to take Dale Carnegie's advice and show some interest. "Are you on a diet?"

She batted her hair out of her eyes. "Are you kidding? I would never do that to myself."

The bell rang. We traded awkward good-byes and lost each other in the crowd.

After my viola lesson on Friday, I abandoned my backpack and instrument on the front steps and rushed to the mailbox. Credit card offers, catalogs, Mom's *Good Housekeeping* magazine. I fanned the pages of the Costco coupon book. Nothing.

What if Kade had decided we weren't the friendship type?

I couldn't blame him. Zoe was flippant, Nora skeptical, and I hadn't added much of anything to the conversation. Boring, he probably thought. I wished I'd shown more interest.

Up in my bedroom, I booted up my laptop. One new e-mail, an offer to get medication from a Canadian pharmacy.

I signed on to Facebook and noticed that my old best friend had updated her status only fifteen minutes earlier.

Sofie Sobol 20 minutes late and my mom won't let me see Jason for 2 weeks! What a WITCH.

Underneath the post, twelve "friends" had already offered sympathies. I didn't know seven of them.

I minimized the screen and flipped open the latch to my viola case, reaching into a compartment for a rag. I polished the varnish until it shone, then tucked my viola under my chin and began Brahms's Sonata in E-flat Major.

As I played, I thought about the time I'd invited Sofie over for our first sleepover since the move—in October, a week before she turned seventeen. We decided she'd take the two-hour bus trip each way, and I'd pay for the round-trip ticket as a birthday present.

When I told Mom, she said, "I know you miss your friend, but I wish you'd try harder to make new ones at Kennedy. Is there another person you could invite to join you?"

I knotted my arms over my chest. "I can't ask a total stranger to come to my sleepover."

"Well, I know, but you could—"

"Mom . . ."

"I get it. Butt out, right? It's just that—"

"You're right," I interrupted. *About butting out.* "I'll try harder. To make friends, I mean."

She picked up the TV remote and tossed it into the basket beside the recliner. "OK, deal."

I didn't know what the deal was, and frankly, I didn't care. Sofie was coming over, and that was all that mattered.

The first thing I did was take down the Chronicles of Narnia movie poster that Mom had taped to the back of my door, replacing it with a picture of Sofie and me the last time we'd trick-or-treated. I'd been a "cereal killer," with a bunch of Cheerios boxes glued to a T-shirt splattered with ketchup. Sofie was supposed to be a rabbit, but when I showed up at her house, her mother was wigging out. Turned out she was a Playboy Bunny.

An hour before Sofie was supposed to arrive for the sleepover, I had grabbed a book and was waiting by the door. At a quarter to seven, every cell in my body was tuned to sounds from outside: high heels clacking on the flagstone, Sofie on her phone, letting her mom know she'd arrived safely, a soft knock on the door.

At seven, I speed-dialed her cell. No answer.

At 7:30, I went online.

At 7:31, Sofie signed onto Facebook.

Charlotte Brody where r u?

Sofie Sobol i wrote you an email. Didn't u get it?!

I switched over to my account.

Subject: So, So Sorry!

I braced myself, then opened it.

Charlotte,
I have a huge test on Monday. I thought I'd be done
studying for it, but it's just too much. We'll get together
soon, promise!

How could my best friend have chosen *studying* over me? But in my heart, I knew it was an excuse. She was moving on.

With memories of Sofie haunting me, the Brahms Sonata felt more depressing than usual. The somber notes and sluggish rhythms did nothing for my mood. When I reached the last note, my phone rang. Nice finale.

I lowered the viola to my lap and answered it. "Hello?"

"Hi, Charlotte. This is Nora."

"Hey," I said.

Silence.

"What's up?" I asked.

"Have you heard anything, you know, about getting together or whatever?"

Nora Walker, queen of vocabulary, sounded inarticulate. It was unnerving.

"Nope, I haven't." All at once, the worries and insecurities I'd tamped down sprung to the surface. "Maybe Kade doesn't want to do it anymore. I don't know, like he's decided it's not worth it, or he wants to find other people."

People who aren't us, I almost said.

"Well, what did he expect?" She sounded like her vocal cords had been sandpapered. "He threw a lot of shit at us."

I was shocked by her use of a pedestrian curse word.

"True," I finally said.

"OK, so I'm intrigued," she admitted. "The whole League thing . . . it's different. Kind of crazy, but at the same time, it's . . . well, anyway, I just wanted to check in with you."

"Thanks," I said. And because I felt like I should: "You know, maybe we can be friends, even if there isn't a League."

"Yeah, sure," she said, her voice distant. That's when I got it: this wasn't about friendship. She was intrigued by the mystery of it all.

As for me, I was already addicted to the adrenaline that had pumped through my veins when Kade looked at me. The withdrawal sucked. Still, friends would be a nice bonus. Since the move, it felt like I'd been shipwrecked on an island—even though technically the island had 1,300 kids on it.

"It was nice meeting you, Charlotte," Nora said. "Call me if you hear anything, OK?" She hung up.

I held the phone in my lap, willing it to ring again. This time it would be Kade, inviting me to another League meeting.

A minute passed. The phone stared back at me.

I returned my viola to its velvet-lined home. A coffin, I

thought. It wasn't until I deposited my new rosin in the upper compartment that I found it, folded into a fat square.

Dear Charlotte,
Please join us on Monday night at 6:00 at a warmer location—329 Main Street, fifth floor. The League needs you!

—K.

♪ CHAPTER 3 ♪

I TOLD MOM THAT I HAD TO WORK ON A HISTORY PROJECT with a friend. If I told her where I was really going, she'd ask a hundred questions that I couldn't begin to answer.

"But it's five thirty, Charlotte! You haven't had dinner yet."

"I grabbed a snack."

"Can't it wait until tomorrow?"

"No," I told her. "I'm not even hungry."

She paused, my words sinking in. "You have a new friend?"

"Not really. It's just a girl. The teacher put us together."

"Could this person become a friend?"

I groaned, rolling my eyes for emphasis. She backed off. "There's salad in the fridge. Take some," she said.

I shook my head, my ponytail swatting the air like a horse trying to get a fly off its tail. "OK, fine." I opened the fridge, stuck my hand in, and plucked out a tomato.

"Charlotte!"

I looked at her innocently. "I have to go."

She heaved a dramatic mother sigh. "So what's this assignment about, anyway?"

"Um, it's a debate. I'm on the side that thinks Senator McCarthy was an ass."

"Watch that mouth," she warned.

I snatched my coat and was halfway out the door when she called out, "He was, actually."

I looked over my shoulder.

"An ass," she clarified. "Be home by nine."

I gave her a big, rewarding grin and stepped out into the startling cold night.

Kade stretched his lanky frame across a king-size bed smack in the center of the studio apartment. "You have no idea how happy I am to see you all."

The other members sat cross-legged on the floor, looking up at him like toddlers on the first day of preschool. The only thing missing were carpet squares. I glanced at the sole chair in the room, stationed by a window. Zoe patted the space next to her and shifted over to make room for me.

"Welcome to the League of Strays," Kade said.

Nora gawked at him like he was the Messiah. I couldn't really blame her. I'd found myself staring at him once or twice or twenty times. Kade was good-looking, which was as much of an understatement as saying that Joshua Bell can play violin. His eyes were the same shade of blue as the waters of the Virgin

Islands, framed with dark eyebrows that made his gaze seem even more potent.

"This group is a puzzle. If a piece was missing, it wouldn't work." Kade spoke with a confidence that was impossible to ignore. He could probably be friends with anyone he chose, if only he wasn't so . . . *intense*. Yep, that was it, from the statement-making hair to the way he commanded the room without saying a word. I bet some people couldn't deal with his intensity. I liked to think I wasn't one of them.

I stole looks around Kade's tiny apartment whenever I had the chance. There were almost no cabinets. Everything from cooking pans to shampoo was lined up neatly, in plain view. Kade's shower was a part of the kitchen, as visible as the refrigerator. Only a chipped white toilet in the closet-size bathroom offered any privacy.

My eyes stopped at the mahogany desk in the corner. Kade owned every imaginable device known to man. An homage to Apple, I thought, as I took in the MacBook Pro with an enormous monitor, iPad on a stand, and an iPod touch resting in the docking station of a bullet-shaped speaker.

"What happened to your parents?" Nora jumped right to the point. She was either refreshingly direct or hopelessly tactless, I hadn't made my mind up yet. I just hoped Kade wouldn't feel forced to delve into some horrifically painful story.

"Just your typical nasty divorce," Kade said, reaching for a bag of potato chips. "You know, spiteful custody battle. Lawyers who pay off their law school debt with my future inheritance. That sort of thing."

"His uncle owns the building. He lives upstairs," Richie said.

"It was ludicrous, all the time my parents spent arguing over who wouldn't get me," Kade told us. "But my uncle said as long as I didn't throw any loud parties or burn the place down, I could crash here."

I was so stunned, I had to tell myself to close my mouth.

"He's the perfect guardian because he leaves me alone," he added, popping a chip into his mouth. "Uncle Ron has a very demanding dating schedule."

"You mean you live by yourself, like all the time?" I asked incredulously.

In a million years, I couldn't imagine my parents letting me have such freedom. But then it occurred to me that in a few months, they wouldn't have a choice. I'd be off to Barrymore, I hoped. For some reason, the thought made my shoulders seize up. I reached up to massage my trapezius muscle, a tip I'd learned in the performance-anxiety elective I took over the summer at Walden Park Conservatory Camp.

"We have dinner together every Sunday. I give him what he needs for the 'parental report,' and everyone's happy." Kade edged toward the foot of his mattress. Closer to me.

"How long have you lived like this?" Nora asked.

"A year."

"If I were your parents, I wouldn't let you out of my sight," Zoe piped in.

"Why do you say that?" He looked sincerely interested. Not the least bit offended by Zoe's remark.

She squinted as if she was trying to see him clearly. "I don't know. You look like the rebellious type."

Kade laughed heartily. "I have a list of therapists who'd agree with you."

Personally, I didn't get Zoe's attitude. She acted like she didn't want to be here, but here she was, parked beside the rest of us.

I guess Kade was thinking the same thing. "You came here tonight, Zoe. Why?"

Nora answered. "You piqued our curiosity."

Kade reached for a can of Coke on his bedside table and gave it to her. She hadn't asked for it, but she took it, anyway.

"I'll assume by your presence that you're all interested in joining the League," he said. "I hope so. The thing is, I know you a little better than you know me, and I don't think that's fair. It's important we're on equal ground."

I, for one, was eager to learn more about Kade Harlin. He was like a good mystery novel; you couldn't turn the pages fast enough.

"I'm going to ask you to do something very difficult," he said. "Zoe, if it makes you uncomfortable, I totally understand. No hard feelings. You can walk out of here right now. But I hope you won't, because I really like your fire. I haven't met anyone like you before, and I think that's pretty amazing."

Zoe's fire expressed itself in a blush. "OK, I'll stay. Just remember, I don't get naked for anyone."

I laughed. One thing about Zoe, she was impressive under pressure. As for me, I could barely form sentences when Kade talked to me.

He swung his feet to the floor and offered her a hand. She hesitated a moment, then reached out to slap it. "You've got my attention," she said. "Continue."

"I want us all—me and Richie, too—to share the worst thing that anyone's ever done to us. I'm asking you to be honest. To take a risk. We can trust each other, I promise."

Nora looked doubtful.

"Tell them the terms," Richie chirped.

"Right, thanks." Kade rolled up the sleeves of his sweater, revealing an impressive pair of forearms. He moved to the floor, beside me. "Whatever we say in this room stays here. If a single word gets out, then the guilty party has to leave the group."

"Dramatic," Zoe mumbled under her breath.

"This is *way* more interesting than studying for trig," Nora said.

Kade had a single dimple on the left side of his face that seemed out of place among his resolved features. He caught me looking and winked. A jolt of electricity zipped through my veins. "Charlotte, you with me?"

If only, I thought. "Oh, um, OK."

Zoe was silent. When she exhaled, I realized I'd been holding my breath, too.

"I know it's hard to trust a bunch of strangers when so many people have let us down," Kade told her. "But that won't happen here."

"Be honest, huh?" She pretended to think about it. "I guess I could try something new."

Kade's laugh was deep and throaty. "You want me to go first?" He looked at us until I nodded. "OK, it happened in the ninth grade. I was in love with this girl in my art class."

In love?

"Who?" Nora asked.

"You wouldn't know her. It was a different school."

"What school?" Zoe said.

I knew somehow that Kade wouldn't answer her, like he had rules for us that didn't apply to him. "The school I went to before Kennedy," he said. "Anyway, she was beautiful—tall, thin, with wavy brown hair." He tapped me on the wrist and shivers rippled up my arm. "She looked a little like you, Charlotte."

Without realizing it, my hand drifted to my hair. Beautiful, like me? I mean, it's not that I thought I was ugly. Funny-looking, maybe. Too tall. Too thin. I let go of my hair, and a curl snapped back like a spring.

"Oh. Um, thanks," I said. *For what, Charlotte, thanks for what?* He hadn't exactly said I was beautiful. I cursed my automatic impulse to be polite.

"I wrote poems about her and left them in her art locker. Every day, I checked to see if she'd written back, but she never did." His gaze drifted to a spider spinning a web over the heating vent. "I memorized her schedule so I could learn everything there was to know about her. She liked egg-salad sandwiches, and her favorite perfume was a five-dollar bottle of Forever Yours that she stole from Walmart. She'd had six boyfriends in the past two years. I even knew the shortcut she took to get home."

Kade sure liked to research people. I rubbed the goose bumps on my arms, but since it wasn't cold in the room, it didn't help. Fear and fascination played tug-of-war inside me.

"I sent her four poems." A look of enchantment, then agony, flashed across his face, and his eyes fluttered shut. "'My hands, like water, flow down your sides, pouring into places unexplored.'"

My face heated up like bad sunburn. *Places unexplored?* A few seconds passed before I realized I was imagining his hands on my body, going exactly where they wanted to.

Kade opened his eyes, but they were lost in the past. "'I seek the inner, the warmth, the soul of you . . . a mingling of spirits. A dance of bodies. A reflection of desire.'"

Desire.

His eyes slid toward me, slow as spilled syrup. "'Mirrored images, unifying into a flame that licks the walls of my chest. Hot with passion promised.'"

I pulled back as if I'd been literally singed by his words.

"Wow," Nora whispered. "Um, that was . . ."

She didn't finish, but Richie nodded like he agreed. Zoe, I noticed, made a point of folding her arms across her chest as if she'd heard better.

"You really liked her," I said in an attempt to show sympathy. I felt like an idiot as soon as it came out. What I really wanted to ask him was, *Could you ever like me that way?*

"I waited a long time for her to respond. Almost a week." His fingers pressed into his knuckles until they popped. "And then one day, she did. Bitch."

His anger was sudden and unexpected, causing my breath to hitch in my throat. We all bent forward, waiting to hear more.

"What happened?" Nora asked breathlessly. She reached into her purse and pulled out a pack of tissues. That's when I noticed the lone tear traveling down Kade's cheek.

"I'm so sorry," he said, his voice cracking. "It still hurts, after all this time. Anyway, she made copies and taped them to classroom doors, the cafeteria wall, school-bus windows. At the top of each one, she wrote, 'By Kade Harlin' in her fat bubble writing."

"What a jerk," I whispered.

"That's the truth," Richie said.

"She moved away a month later," Kade said, staring hard at the wall over my head.

"Good riddance," Zoe offered.

"She left because of me," Kade said.

I wanted to know why, but I didn't ask. Kade had laid his heart at this girl's feet, and she'd stomped all over it. If it had been me, I would've loved to get a poem like that, to have someone care enough to write it.

I guessed that was the end of his story, because he reached for a square pillow on the bed and tossed it to Nora.

♪ CHAPTER 4 ♪

NORA STARED AT THE PILLOW AS IF SHE'D NEVER SEEN ONE before in her life. Adjusting her John Lennon glasses, she said, "So what do you want to know?"

Her blond pageboy haircut framed a sulky face. I still wasn't sure I liked her, but Kade had made the call. I had to trust it was for a good reason.

When he didn't answer, she forged ahead. "Well, as you know, I was a definite for valedictorian until a few months ago. I don't think anyone really appreciates the intense amount of work it takes. I'm the one who studies for tests while everyone else has a life. I'm the one who has to give up extracurricular activities to carve out more time for schoolwork. If I get a lousy grade, I'm screwed. Valedictorians can't afford mistakes."

A part of me admired Nora for her hard work. The other part thought she was crazy for trying. I'd made a resolution to get straight A's once. It lasted about two weeks until I realized that sleep deprivation wasn't my thing.

"I used to have a 4.375 GPA. Then came the ludicrous PE requirement. I rearranged my schedule so I could get Mrs. Cunningham. She gave A's to anyone with two feet. But the first week of class, she tripped over a soccer ball and broke her leg." She groaned dramatically. "So they brought in her replacement. A frustrated, wannabe dancer to teach jock sports, can you believe it? *Madame*, she called herself. No last name, just *Madame*."

"I bet she's from Detroit, not *France*," Richie mumbled. His head jerked up in surprise when I laughed.

"Madame Detroit. A good name for a poseur," Kade said.

"Yeah, well, Madame Detroit had it in for me from the beginning." Nora paused, waiting.

I was the one to give in. "Why?"

"She assumed I picked the class because it was an easy A."

"You did," I said. She shot me a look and I backtracked. "But that doesn't give her the right to pick on you."

Nora forgave me with a smile, then tucked a lock of hair behind her silver frames. "I tried, believe it or not. When she said run, I ran. When she said shoot, I shot. I always showed up, which was better than some of the other kids in the class. But I couldn't get my grade above a C minus. When I went to see her, she had the nerve to say, 'Try harder, *dahling*. Athletics is about zee effort.'"

Richie laughed at the imitation, then covered his mouth with his hand.

Nora frowned. "It wasn't funny. I'm waiting to hear from Stanford. Do you know what a C minus could do to my chances for admission? I mean, my mother went to Stanford, my dad's father, my aunt. It's a family tradition. I've gotten a pair of Stanford PJs every Christmas since I was born."

Wow, talk about pressure. Her parents had her future all wrapped up with a shiny bow before she was old enough to say thank you.

"Now it's just up to me," she added.

Kade shook his head in disbelief. "After six AP classes, including physics and British lit, it must've really sucked that something as stupid as a gym class could pull you down."

I looked around to see if anyone else had noticed his familiarity with Nora's academic history, but they didn't seem fazed. Or maybe they'd already accepted that he knew everything.

"That stinks," Richie agreed. He drew his legs to his chest, echoing Kade's movements.

"My parents were horrified with the grade and even more disgusted when I couldn't get it changed."

"It's just one bad grade," I said. "I'm sure Stanford doesn't expect perfection. It was only a dumb gym class, right? Not something important like calculus."

Nora gave me a look that seemed to say, *What do you know about getting into a top-notch college?* "It's more than that, OK? My parents are busy people. They don't have time for high school drama. As long as I follow the program, everything's copacetic."

"Will they love you less if you don't do well?" Kade asked.

Nora looked disturbed by his question. "That's not what I

mean. It's complicated, with my sister's suicide and all. I don't see any reason to add to their unhappiness."

"But it wasn't your fault," Richie said.

Nora rolled her eyes. "Of course not. It was her idiotic decision. But now it's my job to keep things smooth around the house. My parents are hardly ever around, anyway, but when they are, we don't waste time arguing over report cards."

"That's because you do well," Kade said.

Nora nodded. "Exactly." Then she blinked twice, her mouth pulling into a frown. She looked like she wanted to say more. Instead, she picked up the pillow and flung it like a Frisbee. It spun through the air, landing at my feet.

♪ CHAPTER 5 ♪

ALL EYES WERE TRAINED ON ME. I HUGGED THE PILLOW TO my chest and dove in, with no clue where I was going to land.

"It was hard leaving my friends when I moved . . ." I let the last word linger for Kade's benefit. The common factor among all of us, as far as I could see, was that we were loners. I wanted Kade to know that at least for me, it was by circumstance only.

"Do you guys know Tiffany Miller?" I asked.

Groans and somber nods all the way around.

"She used to go to my old school, about an hour and a half from here. The only good thing about moving was leaving Tiffany behind. Except she followed me to Kennedy. Well, not really, but her family moved here right after mine. Pure nightmare coincidence." I cleared my throat. "It started when I was six, I think. She and her friends used to follow me home from school. They talked behind my back like I wasn't there, and it just got worse."

"How?" Nora asked.

"I had to wear this back brace in the seventh and eighth grades, and I could only take it off in—"

"Scoliosis," Nora said. "Three out of a hundred teens get it."

I rolled my eyes just a bit, but she caught it.

"I read too much," she admitted.

"I know where you're going with this," Zoe told me. "I had a feeling the girl was a loser."

"She called me Hunchback every day," I said.

"What did your parents do?" Nora asked.

I paused at the unexpected question. "I don't know. I didn't tell them."

If I had, they would have said something lame like, "Sticks and stones will break your bones, but names will never hurt you." When that didn't work—because it didn't—Mom would have set up a meeting with the teacher. After that, she'd call Tiffany's parents. Then the principal. Adults were hung up on bullying, but in the end, they usually made things worse. At least, my mother did. She could chop my social life to bits faster than a wood chipper.

Zoe patted me on the back, imitating the generic parent. "Don't worry, dear. Tiffany behaves that way because she's jealous of you."

"They forget how hard school is the second they graduate," Nora added.

Kade looked unimpressed. "What else did she do?"

I hesitated, afraid that if I gave more examples, it would only show that I was a coward, unable to stand up to Tiffany. I didn't want them to think of me as the victim type, whatever that was. Besides, reliving these memories was like pouring rubbing alcohol on a skinned knee. But Kade wanted to know more. The last thing I wanted to do was disappoint him.

"You can tell us anything, Charlotte." His fingers brushed against my knee, light as a fallen leaf.

I rooted through my memory for something more dramatic. "There was one time in fifth grade when Tiffany sent this boy a letter, begging him to be my boyfriend. She signed my name to it. The next day he told me he'd rather eat maggots than get near me."

Back then, I thought I'd never be able to face school again. But here, right now, it seemed like nothing more than an immature stunt. Not bad enough to qualify for lasting-humiliation status. Maybe it *had* been kid stuff. I probably should've let it go a long time ago.

My eyes drifted to Kade's hand, resting on my knee. He didn't want to hear kid stuff.

"Then this other time, she stole my sneakers out of my locker and rubbed them in dog crap. I threw them away and told my gym teacher I'd forgotten them. He made me pick up trash around the jogging track for the rest of the period."

Kade returned his hand to his lap. His face said, *Come on, Charlotte, is that all you've got?*

I glanced around. Everyone was waiting for the climax: my dark, untold secret. But what was it? The truth felt childish. I had to come up with something big, something that would make them feel sorry for me.

Kade's eyes skirted over Nora, who was staring into her cup, deep in thought about something other than my boring story. She was probably thinking about her tragic family. Workaholic parents, academic pressure, suicide—bigger stuff than my childhood teasing.

I wanted Kade's hand back on my knee. I took a breath and, like any good story, started with a seed of truth. "Tiffany and I were in orchestra together at my old school. She played clarinet, but only because she had the hots for this French horn player." Details make a story leap to life, my ninth-grade English teacher used to say. "Derek Logan," I tacked on. I hadn't known the guy's real name, but the made-up one popped into my head as if it had always been there. "We were at an audition for All-State Orchestra. I knew if I landed principal chair, my application to Barrymore would be a lot stronger."

Kade sighed, a little puff of air that urged me to get to the point quicker, whatever the point was. I closed my eyes, transporting myself back to the practice room, to the chaotic mix of scales leaking through the supposedly soundproof door.

"Right before my audition I got thirsty, so I looked for a vending machine. Tiffany was on the floor in the hallway, draped over the guy." All true. But still, uneasiness sat in my stomach at the detour coming up.

What really happened was that the boy's French horn had been lying on the floor, discarded, not even in its case. Tiffany was spelling out words on his palm with an insanely long fingernail. She'd glanced up and said, "Here comes our virginal viola player. I wonder what she uses that bow for?"

It was a stupid comment, and I'd stood there, searching my brain for a retort. Angry at my stalled thoughts. Why did she have to be in my space, my world, spoiling everything? She shouldn't have even been at All-State auditions; she couldn't pull more than a gurgle from her clarinet.

Then they called my name, which meant it was my turn to audition. Without saying anything, not a word of defense, I'd skidded down the hallway, back to the practice room to get my viola.

"And?" Kade asked. "What happened?"

They all leaned forward like flowers bent to the sunlight. Richie, with his arms squared on his knees; Nora, eyes drifting up like she was visualizing scenarios in her head—ones much worse than reality. Zoe, shaking her head as if Tiffany had already let her down. And Kade's almond-shaped eyes, gliding across all our faces, taking it in.

I wondered what they would think if they knew the truth; that my emotions had swirled through my head, then sunk like a boulder to my hands, making my vibrato heavy and unbalanced; that I couldn't latch on to a reliable rhythm; that the notes had come out sharp and flat and everywhere in between. All because Tiffany had glanced at me wrong.

I couldn't admit this to the League of Strays. I had to come up with *something* recruitment-worthy. Enticed by the captivation in their faces, I invented a different ending. "I was confident and prepared when I went into the audition, but a few measures in, my tuning pegs slipped. I asked if I could start over, but it kept happening. Again and again."

"I bet that was frustrating," Kade said, anticipation glimmering beneath a sympathetic look.

"It was," I agreed. "I couldn't stop the tears. Couldn't even see the sight-reading piece they put in front of me." I was surprised at how fast the lie grew. It started out as a quartet and ended up a full orchestra, kettledrums and all.

Something brushed against my shin. *Kade's foot.* A colossal heat wave barreled through my body. Courage welled up inside of me, pushing the words from my mouth. "The judges said they'd heard enough. The 'sorry' letter came in the mail a few weeks later. I hadn't even made the Dungeon . . . that's what they call the last row."

Zoe's hand slid across the floor, her pinkie tapping mine. An act of solidarity coming from her, of all people. She saw my double-take and laughed.

"What happened to your viola?" Nora asked.

"There was something sticky on my tuning pegs," I said. "Peach moisturizer." Peach moisturizer! It was the perfect detail. And *so* Tiffany. She was always pulling those sample-sized bottles out of her purse.

Richie paused, the implication sinking in. "Oh, man."

Nora pinched her nose. "Say no more. I can smell her a mile away."

Kade and Richie smiled at me, and I smiled back. Not because Nora was funny or empathetic, but because I'd survived my own lie.

"Tiffany Miller ruined my dreams," I added, wiping the sleeve of my shirt at a tear that wasn't there.

"That was cruel," Richie said, shaking his head. Nora and Zoe added grunts of disgust.

I felt pleased that my performance could inspire outrage. At the same time, I was stunned by my outrageous performance. The lie sat in my stomach like a clump of dough.

"Does she still bother you?" Richie asked.

"Not lately," I admitted. "I guess she's moved on to more important things."

Zoe snorted. "Like dyeing her hair twelve different shades of Clairol."

"Or making out with the entire lacrosse team behind the gym," Nora said.

Kade's hand was back. An inch higher this time. His fingers were beautiful, long and lean like a professional pianist's. "Someone should teach her a lesson," he said. "Show her how it feels to be humiliated, to have her dreams smashed to pieces."

Did this mean he finally understood that they were, in fact, my dreams? I smiled at the small victory, but Kade read my reaction differently. "That would feel good, wouldn't it, Charlotte?"

The funny thing about Kade was that most of his questions came out like facts. Before I could think more on this, his hand crept a little higher.

I flipped the pillow onto Zoe's lap.

♪ CHAPTER 6 ♫

"I HATE WANDA HARRIS," ZOE BEGAN.

Wanda had been in my choir class last semester. Or at least I think she was. She came and went like a mosquito on a summer day. Most of the time, she hung out behind the tennis courts, keeping cigarette companies in business. The janitor once found purple cigarette butts on school grounds, an exact match to the lipstick on Wanda's big mouth. When our principal, Mr. Reid, questioned her, she called him an asshole to his face. Or at least that's what she told anyone who'd listen.

"She's done a lot of shit to me," Zoe said. "But there was this one time when I thought we could actually stop being at each other's throats."

"Why were you at each other's throats?" I asked.

"Why does Tiffany make your life miserable?" she volleyed back. "Because she can."

It wasn't a stretch to see Wanda in the same light as Tiffany.

The difference was, people didn't mess with Zoe. I'd seen them clear a path when she plowed down the hallway.

"People like that don't need a reason," Kade said. "They're evil."

Evil seemed a little strong, but I didn't want to contradict him. His brows were knit together in a scowl. He looked almost dangerous, in a sexy kind of way. Without warning, he locked eyes with me. Note to self: Stop. Staring. At. Kade.

"So we're both in detention after school," Zoe said, "and Wanda tells me she's having a party. The whole school's coming, she says. I think she's about to go, 'Everyone but you, ass wipe,' but she doesn't. What she says is, 'Let's bury the hatchet, Zoe. Come to my party.'"

I wondered what the hatchet was that needed burying.

"I'd never been to a party before. I mean, it's not like my dance card runneth over, you know? Hey, it sounded good. Real good. So I took the address she gave me and showed up. There was music blasting out of the house and voices laughing. The door was open a crack, so I went in. But there were only guys there. Not guys from school. Older ones." She paused, blinking hard like there was something in her eye.

Richie bit his lower lip. I looked away, knowing that Zoe didn't want us to see her cry.

"Go on," Kade urged.

I took in her panic-stricken expression. "Maybe she could do this later?" I suggested.

Kade cupped his chin in his hand. Waiting.

A tear escaped, rolling down Zoe's cheek. She caught it on

the tip of her tongue and swallowed the evidence. "They were ready for me."

Ready for her? Pangs of sympathy shuddered through my body. I held my breath, mortified.

"'This is a gift from your buddy, Wanda,' one of them said. He grabbed me, tossing me to another guy, then another, and another. Like a basketball, their hands going all over me, everywhere."

Her face tightened, lips a pale, thin line.

"She set you up," Kade said.

"One of them unzipped his jeans while the others watched, cheering him on. I took advantage of the moment and delivered a round kick to the balls of the guy nearest me. They were so busy oohing and aahing in sympathy that I ran out the door. One of them ripped the shirt off my back, but I pulled harder and got the hell out of there."

Her eyes dropped to the mud-colored tank top under her camouflage jacket. "I liked that shirt. Sucks that they trashed it."

Kade slammed a fist down on an empty Coke can, flattening it like an accordion. We all jumped. "Like I said, *evil.*"

This time, I couldn't disagree with him.

Richie leaned across Nora and lifted the pillow from Zoe's lap.

♪ CHAPTER 7 ♪

AFTER A CHEETOS BREAK, RICHIE SCRATCHED HIS HEAD, leaving a few strands of hair pointing up. "Everyone knows my story already."

"Not your side of it," Kade said. "Here's where you set it all straight."

Richie gave him a plaintive look but did as he was told. "Two years ago, I got suspended for bringing drugs to school."

"Is it true you were selling at the middle school?" Nora asked the question on my mind. Probably on everyone's mind.

The way I'd heard it, the cops found a list of names in Richie's wallet. Some of the kids were only in the sixth grade.

"No way," Richie answered. "Dave Harper wanted me to ask my brother Tony for some weed. See, Tony was friends with this jerk named Eddie, who always had a supply. Anyway, Dave kept passing me notes in class, begging me to give him some. He wouldn't stop. So one day, I went into Tony's room, searched through his desk, and found his stash." He pressed his lips together like he'd already said too much.

I felt sorry for him, even though it was stupid to do a favor for a creep like Dave Harper.

"Mr. Reid caught Harper smoking it in the locker room," Kade said. "Took Harper about ten seconds to rat on Richie."

"He told Reid I pressured him to buy it," Richie said.

"Tell them why you did it, why you gave him the drugs," Kade instructed.

Richie's ears matched the color of the smashed Coke can in front of him. "I guess I kind of liked him. I thought maybe . . . maybe he liked me back . . ."

I ran my fingernail along a groove in the scratched-up wood floor, unable to meet Richie's eyes. I knew he was gay—everyone did—but it was hard to listen to something so . . . private. It was weird, all of us spilling our secrets like this. At least no one had laughed or made fun of anyone else. Actually, it was kind of a relief to talk about things I'd kept locked up inside for so long, even if I had taken certain liberties with my story. This is what friends do, I told myself, they *talk*. I couldn't remember the last time I'd had a real conversation with Sofie.

"I was an idiot," Richie said with unexpected ardor. "I trusted everyone. I trusted Dave, without even knowing him. I should've listened to Kade. He knew what a jerk Dave was! He tried to warn me, but I wouldn't listen."

Kade slung an arm across Richie's shoulder. If I'd blinked, I would've missed Richie's adjustment, the almost imperceptible shift closer to Kade. I was beginning to wonder if he had more than just a bad case of hero worship.

"What about the list?" Zoe asked.

Richie shrugged. "Rumor."

A fly buzzed under my nose, and I waved it away. Kade followed it as it zoomed past Nora's ear, tracking it as he spoke. "At the board meeting, Reid defended his star jock. He said Dave was a good kid with a temporary loss of judgment under pressure. The board didn't know who to believe. Since it was a first offense, they both got suspended. Reid was pissed—he wanted Richie expelled."

"I was out for ten days," Richie said.

"What does Mr. Reid have against you?" I asked him.

"He's one of the biggest bigots in the school." Kade seemed surprised that I didn't already know this.

To be honest, I'd had no idea. Our principal was always in front of the school gym, shaking hands with people coming to after-school events. Mr. Reid seemed to have a smile for everyone. Then again, maybe he was checking to see if kids were drunk or on drugs. Could the caring part be an act?

"But didn't our school just start a gay-straight alliance?" Nora asked.

Kade shrugged. "He'd get rid of it if he could. Trust me, Reid doesn't like anyone who's different from him, which means anyone who isn't straight, white, and boring."

"A few weeks later, Dave and five of his buddies jumped out of the bathroom. They punched me and knocked me to the ground," Richie told us. "Dave called me a homo. He told me that's why he asked me to get the drugs, 'cause he knew I'd give it to him for free."

"He used you," Kade said. "But that wasn't enough for him. He had to prove what a macho dude he was by unleashing his personal pit bulls on you."

"Do they still pick on you?" Nora asked Richie.

"Sometimes, but not as much. Not now that I have a body-guard, anyway."

Kade made a muscle. "At your service."

"Wow, I never heard about any of this," I said, ashamed that I'd accepted the rumors, sized Richie up, and cut him down. Like everyone else.

"No one did," Nora said. "Lies make better stories than the truth."

I looked away, the guilt of dishonesty rumbling through my stomach. I'd dressed up the truth, too—when my own misery had failed to impress.

Without taking his eyes off Nora, Kade slammed a hand to the floor. I startled, shrinking my knees to my chest. Kade lifted his palm to check what was underneath, then flicked the dead fly across the room. "Richie got a concussion," he told us, "and a broken finger, too."

"Mr. Reid found out what they did to me, but they only got suspended for a few more days," Richie said. "Then Kade over-heard Reid talking to Dave Harper." He looked at Kade, waiting for him to take over.

Kade shook his head like he still couldn't believe what had

happened. "I was walking by Reid's door when I heard him say that Richie should've been expelled. He was telling Harper he didn't want Richie's 'kind' polluting our school."

"His 'kind'?" Nora let out a breath. "Whoa."

"He didn't have the balls to say it to Richie's face," Kade said. "That guy has it coming to him. He can't get away with treating people unfairly."

"Sometimes he watches us," Richie added.

"He thinks we're lovers." Kade's lips curled into a seductive smile. "So we give him what he wants." He circled an arm around Richie's waist. Richie grinned and dropped his ear onto Kade's shoulder.

"Look at the charming couple," Zoe said, pretending to snap a picture.

The part that still didn't make sense to me was how Mr. Reid could be such a jerk. Kennedy High was more or less a liberal school. But then Reid *did* seem a bit uptight and old-fashioned. He wore a tie to school every day, even in the summer. He was awkward, for sure—but a bigot?

"It isn't fair," Richie said, lowering his eyes.

Kade slammed the glass in his hand down on the bedside table. "Since when is high school fair?" he asked.

♪ CHAPTER 8 ♪

THE INTENSITY OF THE MEETING MADE THE QUIET DAYS that followed seem painfully dull. In between classes, I searched through my locker, the pockets of my coat, the pages of my books.

No notes. Nothing.

Back in the orchestra practice room during lunch, I tackled Paganini. Thoughts of Kade and the League wove through the less-demanding parts, causing my hand to press down on the strings so hard that they left dents in my fingertips.

By the fourth day of waiting, I was in a downright foul mood. I was on my way to speech class when someone tugged on the hood of my jacket. I wheeled around, prepared to unload on the offender.

Nora leaned out of the language lab. "Hi, Charlotte."

I was shocked at how happy I was to see her. "*Hola, bonjour, and guten tag.*"

"I was just wondering, well, have you gotten any . . . you know, correspondences?"

"You mean notes? No, have you?"

She shook her head. "Nada. OK, well, maybe you could let me know if you do."

"Sure."

A hand clamped down on my shoulder. Kade towered over us. "It's fine to e-mail each other or meet after school, but please don't speak in school."

"Why not?" I asked. Friends who couldn't talk in school? School was when you needed them most.

"I'll explain later. Just trust me."

All I heard was *later*. When? I wanted to ask him. When was *later*?

He released his grip, but his hand stayed on my shoulder. "We'll meet at the bleachers at a quarter to five."

My heart started racing, even though there were four more hours to go. I felt my bad mood slip away like dirty water down the drain.

"Actually, I have two tests to study for, thirty-five pages of reading to do, and an in-depth essay on the value of city curfews for urban teens," Nora said. "But I can find time."

Oh, no, I thought as I reviewed my own schedule. Friday afternoons I had my viola lessons with Mr. Watson. "I don't think I can make it today," I told him. "I've got a private lesson."

Kade's eyebrows shot up. He looked as if he'd never heard of a private lesson before. I was about to clarify that it was for my viola when he said, "OK, Charlotte, we'll have to meet without you."

Meet *without* me? "Could we do it on Saturday or Sunday? I'm free anytime . . ." I blushed, realizing I'd just admitted that I had no plans on the weekend.

Kade plucked his backpack off the ground. "It will never be easy to get us all together if we don't make it a priority." He started to leave.

"No, wait. Maybe . . . maybe I could call in sick this one time." I hadn't missed a lesson with Mr. Watson in months. And people did get sick in February.

"I really want you to be there," he said. His uncompromising gaze caused my heart to leap in my chest.

"OK. See you then," I whispered.

"Great!" He smiled and the dimple on his cheek made a special appearance.

When he was out of earshot, Nora said, "Hot one minute. Cold the next."

Mostly hot, I thought, watching him tuck a thumb into his back pocket before fading into the crowd.

"Charlotte, are you with us?" Mr. Holmquist asked.

I forced my eyes to focus. "Uh-huh."

"Let's try again. Would you please identify the cause of the growing distrust between our two characters?"

Which characters? What book? "Not really."

The kids who were still awake snickered.

"Chapter sixteen will definitely be on the final—" The bell killed the rest of his sentence.

I was making my escape when he called out, "Charlotte?"

I muscled my way through the bottleneck at the door, pretending not to hear him.

In front of the library, I pulled out my phone to call Mr. Watson. Thankfully his machine picked up. "Hi, it's Charlotte. I'm not feeling so great. I have a sore throat. And a fever. And I'm pretty sure it's contagious. So anyway, I can't make my lesson today, but I'll practice twice as hard for the next one, OK?"

I went to the choir room to practice Schumann's "Fairy Tales for Viola," hoping it would somehow make up for the lie I'd just told. The piece was mysterious, a perfect match for my mood. Waiting for the League to meet again had been pure torture, and now it was almost over.

Fifteen minutes later, I abandoned Schumann, my thoughts overpowering the music. I stretched out on the piano bench and imagined the kind of poem Kade might write for me one day. I hoped it would be like the one he'd written for that other girl, full of pure desire.

By four thirty, the school was empty. Jocks had showered and left. Detention detainees had been released. On the way to my locker, I saw Nora. I slowed, Kade's warning not to talk in school still hissing in my ears.

We heaved our overloaded backpacks onto our shoulders and headed through the hallways, around the buildings, to the weed-strewn footpath that led to the football field. I didn't say anything to her, not even as I climbed the bleachers by her side.

A minute later, Zoe clomped up the tiers. "Hey, girls!" She dropped into the narrow space between us. "Ready for more intrigue?"

Nora pulled out a fat textbook. She flipped it open, balancing it on her knees. "I've got to study for—"

"He's here," I said breathlessly.

Our heads swiveled to the left like synchronized swimmers. Kade and Richie were cutting a diagonal path up the bleachers. Nora shut her world history book, ditching it in her backpack.

Zoe beat a drum roll on the metal bleachers. With her mittens on, it sounded more like the thud of a bass drum than a snare. "All rise for King Kade and his Royal Representative, Richie!"

"How alliterative," Nora said, rolling her eyes.

I watched them approach, Kade bypassing an entire row with each long-legged step. When he reached the bench below me, he stopped. Richie almost crashed into his backside, then plunked down at Kade's feet.

"Hi, everyone. Thanks for coming."

"Listen, Harlin, about the name, League of Strays. Are you saying we're like a pack of dogs?" Zoe asked.

Nora crinkled her forehead. "Strays? Uh, I have a home."

"Or maybe it's just a house," Kade said.

She leaned back, locking her arms across her chest.

"I've seen you at school, Nora, wandering around, waiting for someone to pat you on the head," Zoe said.

"Whatever." Nora's mouth twitched as she fought a smile.

Kade reached up, scratching her behind the ears. Nora growled, and we all cracked up. I was glad he hadn't done that to me. I might've rolled onto my back with my legs in the air, which wouldn't have been pretty.

"Anyway, I thought that after what I put you through last time, you all might want to ask me some questions," Kade said. "Like a Q-and-A. You ask first, then I get a turn. Sound fair?"

Zoe groaned, but I, for one, was game. What was he going to ask me? And how was I going to wade through the hundreds of questions in my head to pick just one for him?

"So, are you going to come clean with us?" Zoe asked. She tried to stare him down, but her eyes slipped off his face like butter in a nonstick pan.

What did she mean, come clean? True, Kade had a flair for the dramatic, but he'd already told us this was a friendship group. An alternative one, maybe, but sometimes you had to go with the flow. Try something different. And besides, this was more interesting than being holed up in my bedroom, reviewing vocabulary words from *Macbeth*.

Kade didn't ask what she meant. He looked at her, silent and pensive. Nora slid her ring on and off, on and off, on and off. I waited for him to speak, my breath shallow. The air felt as heavy as a humid summer day, even though right now my hands were a patchwork of red from the cold.

Kade's expression melted into laughter, punctuated by Richie's titters. "I guess we have our first question and volunteer. I'll tell you everything you want to know by the end of this meeting, Zoe. I promise. I just need to make sure we're all committed first."

I was confused. Since when did friendship require a formal commitment?

"Definitely," Richie responded. I wondered sometimes if Kade had his arm up Richie's back, making his puppet talk.

"If you could do anything without getting caught, what would it be?" Kade asked Zoe.

She pondered the strange question. "I don't know, um, drop a bomb on Kennedy High?"

I was the only one who cracked a smile.

"God, kidding." Her hair fell over her eyes, and she flicked it back. "Maybe I'd just burn down the school. That seems easier than making a bomb. I'm lousy with Internet instructions."

"I have a question," Nora said. "Why can't we talk in school? I mean, what's the point of having friends if you can't even sit with them at lunch?"

"It's important no one knows we exist. Not as a group, anyway. They need to think of us as single, powerless entities," Kade said.

Powerless? Against what? And who were "they," anyway?

"So Nora, what's pissed you off in the last week?" he asked.

"That you didn't answer Zoe's question," she said. Zoe grunted a laugh, and Nora's eyes flitted back to Kade. He wasn't smiling. "OK, so I found a photo album of my sister and her friends. She made it when she was thirteen. I asked my mother if she'd seen it before, but like always, she changed the subject. The weather was more important, apparently."

"Maybe it hurts too much to talk about it," I suggested.

"Whenever Kelly comes up in conversation, my parents clam up. It's like she never existed." Softly, she added, "Just because she's dead doesn't mean I can forget her, even if I wanted to."

I touched her arm and she flinched, pulling it back. "So who thinks we should be let off campus during lunch? I'm going to start a petition."

As the others discussed it, I silently rehearsed my own question, zeroing in on the part that was most confusing to me.

"Why did you pick us to be in the League?" I interrupted. Maybe Kade really did want friends, but I still didn't get the logic behind this specific roster.

"Because we're perfect together. We're loners. We know what it feels like to be teased, harassed, and ignored." Kade studied me like he was deciding if I was worthy of the truth. I tried to meet his eyes, unflinching. He seemed impressed by my momentary courage, even if we both knew it was an act. "The purpose is to get back at those who deserve it."

I looked around. Nora was taking rapid breaths. Zoe sat on her hands, staring at Kade. Neither of them looked half as surprised as I felt.

"Get back?" I asked. "How?"

"That's for all of us to decide together."

"Who do you think deserves it?" Zoe said.

"Everyone we talked about," Nora said.

"You and Charlotte have something in common," Kade told her. "That PE teacher and Tiffany Miller didn't respect your dreams. They ruined them because they could."

Nora nodded. "They're on a serious power trip."

"People can't get away with bad behavior because they're jealous or in a lousy mood or they want to look cool. Someone has to stop them." Kade made this observation calmly, like most things he said, but I detected a simmering anger behind his words.

"They cut us down so they can look bigger," Zoe noted.

"I'm not going to let Wanda get away with what she did to you," Kade said. I saw a tear glisten in Zoe's eye before she glanced away. Kade guided her chin back with a finger. "Things are going to change for all of us."

I guess I was the only one who'd fallen for the friendship bit. Maybe because I'd wanted it so much. Kade hadn't been shopping for friends; he wanted to make a bigger statement to the jerks of the world. I felt embarrassed for believing that he might actually want to get to know me.

"Charlotte?" Kade was looking at me. Maybe he was afraid I'd bolt. For once, his intuition failed him. I couldn't go anywhere, not with his eyes fastened on mine.

I nodded, doing my best to appear like this new information didn't faze me. Kade brought a fist to his mouth, and I realized he was hiding a smile. I pursed my lips, annoyed that he could read my emotions so effortlessly.

"Don't get me wrong, I chose all of you because I like you," he said. "But I also knew we could right some wrongs together." His eyes were like a drill, burrowing inside me.

"Maybe as a group, we could talk to someone about this. Someone who cares . . ." I found myself suggesting.

"Not our parents," Nora said.

"Or teachers," Richie added.

"They never see what's happening, even if they're standing ten feet away," Zoe said.

"Unless you hit back," Nora said. "Then *you're* the one who gets caught."

"Not if you do it when no one's looking," Kade said.

I turned his words around, looking for a chink in the logic. Revenge was wrong, immature. Everyone knew that. But I also knew that if I said that out loud, Kade would ask me to explain why. And I wasn't sure how to answer.

Nora raised a finger. "As the president's younger brother, whom our illustrious school is named after, once said, 'Don't get mad, get even.'"

"You're a walking encyclopedia, aren't you?" Zoe said.

Nora laughed. "I'm trying to break the habit."

"What about karma? Won't they get their punishment in, like, a spiritual sense?" I reasoned.

"That's just something we tell ourselves to make it feel better," Kade said. "But we can *be* their bad karma, if that's how you want to think about it."

I didn't know what to say.

"We're going to have a great time coming up with creative ways to get our point across," he said, folding his arms on his knees. "I suspect you guys haven't had a lot of fun lately, but you deserve to. And the people who've stepped in your way need to get what they deserve, too."

"Um, does that include teachers?" asked Nora.

I held my breath.

"Madame Detroit can be first, if that's OK with everyone. Then Dave Harper. And Wanda. And we won't forget Tiffany." He winked at me. I glanced away, but when I looked back, his eyes were still on me. "Subtle and swift, Charlotte. I bet you'd like to knock Tiffany off her pedestal."

"I'd like to see that," Nora said.

I nodded, but I wasn't so sure. I didn't make decisions quickly, which had always been my problem. I could see all sides to a story, which made it hard for me to come up with a definite opinion. *She lives in a bubble, her every move dictated by Mommy and Daddy.* Kade had been right: I had no clue how I felt about a lot of things. Not even Tiffany.

Kade straightened, hands intertwined. A king on his throne, surveying his subjects. "So, who's in?"

His face seemed friendly, serene even, as he waited for our response. Like a row of bobbleheads, Richie, Nora, and I nodded.

Zoe didn't move. I half expected one of her protests, but she stared ahead like she was hypnotized. Finally, she said, "What the hell, sign me up. Anything that gets me out of the house is good." You'd think someone had just asked her to join a softball team.

Kade slapped a hand on his thigh. "I knew you guys had it in you! You're awesome. Completely and utterly awesome."

I felt a surge of pride, like when I was younger and my parents gave me double stars on my behavior chart for every A I brought home.

Tiffany was a loser, I thought. Maybe it *would* be fun to return some of the favors she'd given me over the years. If I could only loosen up.

"We're anonymous, but powerful," Kade said, shaking his fist in the air.

"So that's why we can't be seen together," Nora said.

I had a few more questions. "But why—?"

A grin spread across Kade's face. "Answers will come in time, Charlotte. It's my turn now. Ready?"

No, I thought. I wasn't ready for anything he said to me.

"Tell me, do I scare you or thrill you?"

My face went to five alarms. I couldn't speak.

He kept his eyes on me, his tongue darting out to wet his lips. Make that six alarms.

"Truth, Charlotte," Nora reminded me.

I floundered. "You make me nervous. Intrigued, I guess, but nervous."

Oh God, had I really just said intrigued?

"Sounds to me like a love-hate thing," Zoe said.

Richie smirked, and Kade smiled.

"It's like you have multiple personalities," I told him.

The others joined in on his laughter like backup singers. As much as I didn't want to, I smiled at my own assessment. It did sound a tad melodramatic.

"My therapist—a condition my parents made in exchange for an extra hundred per month—says if I don't express my emotions, I could make myself sick. He says it's dangerous for me to keep things bottled up inside."

Kade scaled three more rows of bleachers and sat down. He

leaned back, resting his elbows on the row behind him. I twisted around to see him. "We're going to send a message to the people who need to hear it." His voice was soft as a purr, like he was sharing a secret with me.

Nora's eyes sparked with interest. "What do you have in mind?"

"For starters, Madame Detroit's going to learn that it's not nice to knock down someone's hard work."

"This is really going to happen?" Nora spun a pearl earring in her ear. A tentative smile spread up her face, settling in her eyes. "Really?"

"Um, what if we get caught?" I asked him.

"Stupid people get caught. With our combined brainpower, there's nothing to worry about."

I felt like I was having an out-of-body experience, hovering overhead as the others cheered. I didn't really know what I was signing up for. All I knew was that Kade was part of the package deal, and that was a compelling enough reason to sign on the dotted line. I heard myself agree to meet back, same location, late Sunday night.

At least it wouldn't be hard to get out of the house. My parents would be out cold by ten thirty.

♪ CHAPTER 9 ♫

I JOGGED TO KEEP UP WITH KADE'S LONG STRIDES AS HE stomped through the brush behind Kennedy. A massive tree root gripped my foot and I stumbled, falling to my knees. I cried out, feeling a warm trickle of blood down my leg.

Kade lifted me up as if I weighed nothing. "You're fine."

He was right. With his arm molded to my waist, I felt better than ever.

The sliver of a moon ducked behind the clouds. I could only make out the rocks and sticks right in front of me. I grasped the back of his jacket. He reached around, unhooked my hand, and twined his fingers through mine. His thumb nestled in the crook of my palm.

I closed my eyes, allowing him to lead me. I imagined it was the middle of the afternoon and we were walking down the street together. Like normal friends, hanging out.

We emerged in front of a window at the back of the school.

The glass was new—the window company's sticker still on the pane.

Kade let go of my hand, and the night air swarmed in to take its place, harsh and cold. As I was considering how a hand could feel so lonely, Kade punched his foot through the window. I winced at the explosion of shattering glass, then stared at him. I'd never imagined that we'd actually have to break into the school. With all the hundreds of windows around, I figured there had to be at least one that was open. He hadn't even bothered to check before he'd sent his foot through it.

Kade reached into his jacket and pulled out a pair of cotton gloves from his pocket. He slipped them on and rooted through his other pocket for a bunch of latex gloves. "Make sure you don't touch anything unless you have these on," he instructed, giving each of us a pair. "They'll check for prints."

I stared at the pads on my fingers, tough from nine years of viola practice. Kade thought the police were going to be involved? But of course they were, now that there was a broken window. I imagined them dusting the window frame, searching for clues.

The gloves were a size too big, but I struggled to slip my sweaty hands inside the rubber. Oh God, why had he broken the window? There was no going back now.

Kade kicked at the remaining shards of glass until the rim was clean. Then he rapped on the wooden frame. "Hello? Anyone home?" He turned to me. "After you," he said, as if he were holding the door open at a fancy restaurant.

"No way," I protested. "After you."

"No problem." He swung his legs through the opening and dropped from view. A moment later, he called, "All clear!"

One by one, we shimmied onto the basement floor, glass crunching under our feet. I swept the cobwebs off my jeans.

"This is so cool!" Nora gushed, sidling up to Kade.

Zoe laughed. "We're a bunch of lunatics."

We lined up single-file and moved toward a light that fanned out from under a closed door.

"Wait, what if someone's there?" I whispered.

It can't be the police, I told myself. Not yet. But it could be a janitor. Or a teacher.

"Don't worry, Charlotte," Richie assured me. "They always leave the lights on in the storage room. We have to cut through here to reach the stairwell, and then we'll be right outside the gym."

"How come you guys know so much about breaking into the school?" Zoe asked.

"I like to be prepared," Kade said. "We don't want to stumble around in the dark all night trying to find the gym."

Something scampered across my sneakers. I hopped back. "I, for one, appreciate that. The sooner we're out of here, the better."

We hadn't actually discussed what we were going to do to the gym teacher's office. I hoped it would be quick. Maybe throw a few files around. Empty some drawers. Spill a rack of basketballs on the ground. Then get out.

"Come on, you chickens," Nora called over her shoulder. She pulled the door open.

"No more Miss Perfect," Zoe mumbled under her breath.

"Here's to the new-and-improved Nora," Kade said, taking her hand as they entered the storage room. I stared at their braided fingers. My heart felt squeezed like a stress ball.

The room was stacked from floor to ceiling with boxes of vending-machine food. Kade ripped one open and lobbed snack-size bags of Oreos to each of us. Under the buzz of fluorescent lights, I took a moment to examine myself. My clothes were covered in dust bunnies. Dirt under my fingernails. The blood from my injured knee had soaked through my jeans. I was sure that the damp air outside had turned my curly hair into a web of frizz. I hoped Kade wouldn't look too closely.

I followed behind everyone, groping my way up the dark stairwell, until Kade opened a door, sending welcome shafts of fluorescent light at my feet. "We're here." He stepped into the familiar school hallway.

"Time for fun!" Richie called, his normally meek voice reverberating against the concrete walls. I shrank at the volume. Without the usual bodies in the hallway, there was nothing to soak up the sound.

"It's all right," Kade said, noticing my terrified expression. "Reid's always the last one to leave, and he never works past six. Trust me."

I wondered if he ever missed anything. "My mother says never trust anyone who says 'Trust me,'" I told him.

His hand wound up my arm like a snake. "What do you think, Charlie?"

I frowned, but it was just an act. Secretly, I was thrilled. *Charlie.*

A few times, people had tried to shorten Charlotte that way. I'd always corrected them, but not this time. The way it rolled off Kade's tongue, the nickname took on new luster.

Richie slammed his small frame against the lockers, calling out every bad word in the book. Coming from him, they sounded like endearments. I couldn't help but laugh. One by one, we all started screaming obscenities at everyone we'd ever hated. Or rather, they did. I hadn't been at Kennedy long enough to hate that many people, but their list was longer than the hallway. "I hate you, Tiffany Miller!" I finally screamed.

I turned around to find Kade. His eyes latched on to mine, and he gave a slow, determined nod.

When we reached the double doors of the gymnasium, we collapsed on the floor from post-adrenaline exhaustion. Maybe it was the thrill of breaking and entering, or the power of belonging, or the release of pent-up anger. Whatever. It felt amazing.

Richie offered me a hand, lifting me to my feet as Kade rattled the gym door. It didn't budge. He turned to Richie, who flashed a shiny key in his palm. Kade punched him lightly on the shoulder.

"I borrowed it," Richie told the rest of us, beaming. "It's from Reid's office."

"Oh, great," Zoe muttered. "The cops will be waiting for us on the other side."

I pictured Richie in his red-and-white striped Grant's Drugstore uniform. Two months ago, I'd gone to make a copy of our house key. When I'd seen Kennedy High's drug dealer behind the register, I changed lines.

"He made a copy at Grant's," I guessed. "He probably put the original back."

Kade drew a finger down my back. "Can't pull one past Charlie." He lowered his voice, for my ears only. "I'll have to keep that in mind."

Nora wiggled her way between us. "What are we waiting for, Harlin, a formal invitation?"

Richie inserted the key. After some jiggling, the door clicked open.

ƒ CHAPTER 10 ⎱

ONCE WE GOT STARTED, IT WAS LIKE RIDING A ROLLER coaster with no way to slow down.

Nora took a thick black marker off a cluttered desk and flicked the top across the room. On the whiteboard, she scrawled, *MA DAMN IS A BITCH!*

My mouth dropped open. For my seventh-grade science project, I'd analyzed the effectiveness of various solvents in removing different kinds of ink stains. Nothing had worked on a Sharpie. How much would it cost to replace a whiteboard, anyway? Five hundred? A thousand? Money the school didn't have.

Kade was standing under the doorjamb. I saw him wink at Nora. She leaned against the whiteboard, ankles crossed, and smiled.

Zoe found a penknife in one of the desk drawers and was systematically stabbing some footballs from the supply closet. When she was done mutilating them, she pressed her clunky black boots down until they each exhaled a last breath. Then she flung the rubber pancakes across the room. They whizzed by Richie's head like flying saucers.

As I watched them, Kade snuck up behind me, his body flush against my backside. Manipulating my hands, he plunged them into the recycling bin and tossed the shredded paper into the air. I felt like a rag doll.

Richie launched into "Auld Lang Syne" while confetti streamed down on our heads. After the first line, he la-la-la'd through the rest.

"What a lame song," Zoe said.

"New year, new start." Nora glowed. I'd never seen her look so happy.

"It's February already," I said.

Nora grabbed a book and threw it at me. I ducked. *Techniques for Better Volleyball* slammed against the rear window and slid to the floor.

"You're not even strong enough to crack a window," Zoe teased.

"I am!" Richie hollered. He lifted a postage meter over his head and hurled it across the room. The machine shattered on impact, creating a spiderweb of cracks in the glass. With a light tap from Kade's fist, the pane crashed to the ground. Glass skittered across the floor.

I froze, fascinated and horrified at the same time. My eyes swept over the room, cataloging the damage. It looked like a twister had swallowed everything up, then spit it back out. Hockey sticks snapped in two. A punctured exercise ball drooped over the arm of an office chair. A torn soccer uniform hung from a coat hook like a flag of defeat.

I picked up a small trophy, a sixth-place finish for our less-than-stellar swim team. My eyes drifted up to find Kade in front of me. I started to shake my head, or maybe I imagined I did. No, I didn't do this. I didn't do any of this. But I stopped, trapped in Kade's smile. My arm pulled back and suddenly the trophy was released, flying through the air. It hit a vase of dying flowers, which seemed to tumble in slow motion to the floor. The glass split open and water seeped out into a heart-shaped puddle.

Kade leaned in. "Nice job, Charlie."

I smiled back, relishing the tickle of his breath on my ear.

Zoe waved a navy-blue binder over her head. "Hey, everyone, look at this!"

Nora glanced at the dates on the cover. "Oh my God, this thing goes back three years!" She yanked it from Zoe's hands. After a quick check, she began ripping out pages from the middle.

"Hey, what are you doing?" Kade hissed.

The others stopped, mid-destruction.

"When they look at the torn pages, the suspect list will go from a few hundred to twenty-five," Kade said. "All they have to do is check out the C's and below, and your name will be on a short list."

Nora fanned an arm across the room. "You think someone's going to notice a few missing pages in all this mess?"

"We can't leave any clues." Kade's voice was steely.

"Come on, guys. It's OK," Richie said, palms up.

"Why don't you just destroy the whole book?" Zoe asked.

Kade stepped toward Nora, holding out a hand in what I assumed was a peace offering. She turned her back to him.

Zoe pulled a lighter out of her purse. The wavy blue flame danced under the grade book. A minute later, smoke turned to flame. She dropped it on the floor, and I watched the crisp pages curl to ash. She stomped out the smoldering embers with her boots, leaving a melted hole in the linoleum. "Problem solved," she said.

Richie's snort broke the tension. We fell into fits of laughter until our lungs begged for air. My own laughter had the forced quality of an actor onstage delivering a bad performance. The room looked terrible, worse than I'd imagined. I'd thought we'd throw a few papers around, maybe knock some books off a shelf—nothing like this.

I rested against the wall, spent from the manic act of destruction. A piercing alarm delivered a new dose of adrenaline.

Zoe threw her hands over her ears. "Oh damn, the fire alarm!"

"Let's go," I cried. I was already out the door, the others on my heels. I flew through the gym, down the hallway, and into the stairwell. The alarm caught its breath, then screamed again.

Back in the basement, I dashed to the window and stepped into the cradle of Kade's hands. He launched me through, and I tumbled, arms flailing, onto the dirt path. I managed to roll out of the way a second before Richie, Zoe, and Nora catapulted outside.

"Come on!" I screamed to Kade as the lights from the fire truck flashed in the distance.

He wriggled out the opening. We scrambled across the unkempt field, not stopping until we were hidden behind a wall of pine trees.

"Holy shit," Zoe said breathlessly as we watched the firemen pry open a door.

"I can't get caught. I can't!" Nora said.

"You won't," Kade told her. The worse things got, the more confident he became. It was comforting to know he wasn't worried, kind of like the moment when the pilot comes on the intercom to tell you that the safety belt light is off.

My eyes drifted down to a bare hand. *Oh, no.*

"My glove!" I cried. "It was just here." I had no idea where I'd lost it. In the field? In the stockroom? *In the gym office?* My fingerprints were in that glove.

"Oh, crap, Charlotte," Nora said, as if I'd done it on purpose.

Kade extracted the missing glove from his pocket and snapped one of its fingers. "No worries, Charlie. I had you covered. I have all of you covered."

I exhaled, relieved, but my heart kept up its double-time tempo.

"Everything went according to plan," he said. "The alarm part was unexpected, but what a finish. Congratulations, everyone!" His smile lit up the night, wrapping me in its warmth.

Richie took the glove from Kade and pressed the opening to his mouth. He blew, expanding the rubber until it looked like a bloated king with a crown on his head. He waved it at us, then let it go. We all laughed.

Kade kneeled down to retrieve the glove. "It was a new moon

a few days ago. That was part of the plan, too. Those firemen couldn't spot us with binoculars."

Nora thought about it, then nodded. "Did you know that in astrology, the new moon means the sun and the moon are aligned in the same sign? Supposedly, an energy portal is opened, or something like that. Anyway, it's a great time for new beginnings."

Kade raised his fist to the moon. "To new beginnings."

We joined ours with his. "To new beginnings," we echoed.

When the distant fire alarm, which had faded into background music, gave a strangled hiccup and cut out, Kade turned his back on the school and strolled away. I took one last look at Kennedy High, bathed in red strobe lights, before going after him.

♪ CHAPTER 11 ♪

I COULDN'T WAIT TO SEE EVERYONE'S REACTION TO THE news, which would probably be all over the school by the time I got there. I hadn't even made it through the parking lot when it started. Kenny York, under the hood of his '74 Camaro, had a cell phone pressed to his ear with one shoulder while fiddling with his engine.

"They did what? In the gym?" He pulled out a screw, studied it, then dropped it into his back pocket. "Christ, dude, for real? Damn, that takes balls."

I turned my head and smiled. I liked being part of the action for once.

My pride came crashing down when I saw the row of teachers lined up like soldiers at the school entrance. They parted to let a few kids in, then moved back into formation. It was a scare tactic—I knew that—but it worked. As soon as I made it through, hall monitors ushered me into the auditorium.

Nora sat in the last row, observing the commotion around her. Her eyes were big and bright as they swept past me, taking in the crowd. They latched onto Mr. Reid as he moved down the aisle to the stage. He pulled a pencil from his blazer and tapped three times on the microphone. Feedback shrieked through the room. The crowd fell silent, as if someone had hit the mute button. Nora's lips curled into a half-smile.

"Can everyone hear me?" Mr. Reid yelled into the microphone. The first two rows covered their ears. "I'm sure by now many of you know that a serious act of vandalism occurred last night. The damage was extensive. A great deal of athletic equipment was destroyed. For those of you taking gym this week, you'll meet in the auditorium for an extra study period until further notice."

Groans erupted from the jock section.

"I can assure you that we'll find the perpetrators," Mr. Reid added, causing the same jocks to cheer.

I swallowed, hoping to dislodge the rock in my throat. Next to the principal, a couple of teachers scanned the crowd, alert for unusual reactions. I wanted to check out Nora again, but I didn't dare take my eyes off the stage.

"I'm asking for your help. If anyone has heard or seen anything suspicious, please report it to me at once. For those responsible, I urge you to turn yourselves in." He gestured toward the back of the room.

Everyone twisted in their seats to gape at the two policemen looking back. Someone dropped a pen. It gathered speed as it rolled down the sloped auditorium. I tried to focus on my breathing. In-out. In-out. In-out. Now would be a bad time to pass out.

"The extent of your punishment will increase with each hour that Officer Price and Officer Henderson spend on this crime." Each cop waved stiffly when Mr. Reid mentioned his name.

Seniors were supposed to do these kinds of things before graduation, I told myself. It was a prank. This would all blow over by the afternoon.

Mr. Reid muttered "Thank you," walked up the aisle, and exited the auditorium, the cops behind him. The noise swelled to a roar as kids pushed out of their rows.

What kind of punishment was he talking about, anyway? Suspension? Payment for damages? Would the cops actually *arrest* us?

Stupid people get caught, Kade had said.

We aren't stupid, I thought to myself, repeating it like a mantra.

A few heads in front of me, slick black spikes bobbed up and down. I wanted to push everyone aside to get to Kade. His disregard for Mr. Reid's dramatics might help me get some perspective.

Behind me, Greg Jacobs, football god of Kennedy High, said, "If I get my hands on those jerks, I'll kick them right through the goalposts."

I tried to muster some anger. If the orchestra room had been vandalized, the jocks would have yawned.

But it was a lot more than a few footballs. I couldn't kid myself.

Greg's sneakers scraped against the back of my heels. I twisted around. "Stop it!"

He and his jock friends looked at me like I'd materialized out of nowhere.

Behind them, Zoe moved up the aisle, her face three shades lighter than the honey-colored skin on her arms.

One thing was certain: we'd found something in common besides our loneliness. The fear of getting caught.

♪ CHAPTER 12 ♩

EXCEPT FOR THE OCCASIONAL COP IN THE HALLWAY AND jocks grumbling because they had nothing to do, life returned to normal. Or at least I hoped so.

Mr. Reid said that the punishment would increase with each hour, and now days had gone by since the assembly. My fear festered and spread, invading my brain. I couldn't think of anything else. If the police questioned us, who would dissolve under pressure and start talking? Not me, that much I knew. My parents would go ballistic if they found out. Kade wasn't going to spill anything; the League had been his brainchild in the first place. Richie didn't sneeze without Kade's permission. But what about Nora? Miss Perfect might crawl into her parents' arms to dump her guilt. She seemed desperate for their attention. Zoe was an unknown, too. She might have a hard outer shell, but inside I suspected she was soft as room-temperature butter.

When the last bell rang, I dumped the contents of my locker into my backpack and flew out the door. Nora had a tutoring job on Thursdays, so by default, I decided to find Zoe. I needed to know how committed she was to the League.

Slow down, Charlotte. People will stare.

I spotted the yellow dumpster stuffed with tar paper at the end of the block. I ducked behind it and took out my phone.

"Hello?" Mom answered.

"Hi, Mom."

"Hi, hon! How was school? Are you calling me from there? You know they don't allow cell phones on campus."

I sighed. "Not in class, but we can use them everywhere else. Anyway, listen, I'm waiting for this girl to help me with calculus."

"Oh, really? Who is she?"

"Just a girl. Anyway, I'll be home in an hour."

"No. No," she said. "Don't rush. Dinner won't be ready for a while. Maybe you can become friends? See if you have any interests in common—does she play an instrument?"

A parade of kids walked past the dumpster. Still no sign of Zoe.

"Oh, there she is! Gotta go, Mom. Bye." I disconnected the call.

I didn't need intricate lies to get out of the house. All I had to do was say the word "friend" and Mom would boot me out the door.

My skinned knee throbbed as I waited, and now my foot

had fallen asleep. As I stomped it on the ground, I caught a blur of military green out of the corner of my eye. I dropped to a crouch and peered around the dumpster.

Zoe was walking down the middle of the street, kicking a soda can. When she passed by, I flicked the grimy pebbles from my jeans and trailed behind her. I felt like a TV cop, darting behind cars in pursuit of an armed criminal. The ambiguous boundaries of Kade's "no talking" rule kept me at a distance.

Zoe slowed in front of a mustard-colored house. Cracked cement scarred the short driveway. Old paint curled from the garage door like banana peels. She stepped over a picket fence that was missing a post and ran up the porch steps. As she fumbled through her backpack for a key, I made my move.

"Um, Zoe?"

She whirled around. "Jesus, Charlotte. You almost gave me a heart attack!"

"Sorry."

"Were you following me?"

"I was on my way to a babysitting job," I lied.

"In West Glenwood? Give me a break. People on this street can't afford babysitters."

I tried to laugh, but it came out like a pig squeal. "It's a few blocks from here."

"Are you in a hurry?"

I shrugged.

"Come on in." She disappeared into the house.

The living room was dark. Shades were drawn over every

window. Zoe zigzagged through the room, snapping each one up. I followed her into the world's smallest kitchen. Dirty dishes filled every inch of counter space. She glanced around, then dove for the empty vodka bottle, stuffing it down into an already full trash can.

I tried to sound casual. "So, what did you think about that assembly?"

She opened the refrigerator. "You mean the one a few days ago?"

As if there'd been another.

"Whatever," she said.

"Do you think Mr. Reid was serious, you know, about hunting us down?"

"Are you kidding? He'll be on to something else soon enough." She held up a yogurt, examined its expiration date, and chucked it into the trash. "Like the cleavage on display with the new cheerleader uniforms. Did you see June Martin today?"

I shook my head.

Zoe burst into a song from *Carousel*, a musical the drama department had performed in the fall. "June is bustin' out all over!" Her arms swayed in the air. She looked pleased when I laughed.

"Why didn't you try out for it?" I asked. "The musical, I mean."

She smirked. "Yeah, right. Do you think they'd let me wear combat boots under my petticoat?"

I shrugged.

"Hey, what kind of host am I? You must want something to drink. We have wine, vodka, or gin and tonic." She laughed at my expression. "Never mind. How about some milk and cookies?"

"Um, no thanks."

"No wonder Kade's got a thing for you. Boys like him get off on your type."

My ears perked up. "Why do you say that?"

"Oh, I don't know. Maybe it's the way he keeps touching you. Boys are such idiots. They want the virginal ones, and when they get them, they realize that's not what they want after all. What they really crave is my type."

I frowned, not sure which part irked me more—that my inexperience was as obvious as my height, or that Zoe believed I couldn't keep Kade's interest.

"What makes you think I'm still a virgin?" Had I really just said that?

She grabbed hold of my shoulders, shaking me like a rattle. "Are you messing with me?"

It was my turn to laugh. "Yeah."

She tromped down the hall to a room that looked more like a barracks than a bedroom. She was the only person I knew who had khaki and green accent colors.

"What's with the army motif?" I asked.

She flung herself onto the bed and walked her feet up the wall. "I have to protect myself. Zoe Carpenter: one-woman unit."

She reached over her head to turn on her iPod. Gospel came

out of a pair of cheap blue speakers. Zoe added her own line of harmony. I couldn't believe it; she sounded great. Soulful, actually.

"Wow, you're really good. Have you thought about voice lessons?"

"YouTube is my teacher," she said pointedly. "The price is right."

I nodded, suddenly embarrassed. Having a conversation with Zoe was like wandering through a minefield.

"What were you saying about Kade?" I asked.

"About him liking the innocent type?"

"No, about him liking me."

She grabbed my hand, pulling it to her chest. "I want your body, Charlie!"

I yanked my hand back, then scooped up the basketball on the floor and threw it at her. It bounced against the wall, rebounding into a picture frame on the bookshelf. I held my breath as the frame clattered to the floor. Luckily, it didn't break. I picked it up and looked at the couple in the photograph: a black man hung an arm across the bare shoulders of a pretty woman with long blond hair.

"Um, are they your parents?" I asked.

Zoe found a handful of darts inside a coffee mug. She hurled them across the room, where they stuck in the wood paneling. "So they tell me. He doesn't even know I exist."

I look at her, confused.

"Mom never informed him that she was knocked up."

Zoe's dad had a perfect, straight nose, a pouty lower lip, and dark eyebrows with a high arch. I could tell that the photo was really old. "You look like him," I said.

"Well, you know what they say. We all look the same."

"That's not what I meant."

She rolled onto her side and extended a hand. "Sorry, Charlotte. Seriously."

"I'm not like that, Zoe."

"Yeah, yeah, I get it," she said. "I don't know why I said that."

From somewhere in the house, a door slammed. "I'm home!"

"Oh, shit." Zoe pulled a blanket over her eyes, then yanked it down again. "Leave through the back door."

I was confused. "Shouldn't I be here?"

Her mom threw the door open and leaned against the door frame. The cascading blond hair was gone, shorn above the ears. "I never thought I'd see the day when you'd bring a little pal home from school." She drawled out the word "pal," holding it like a half note.

"She was just leaving." Zoe dragged me toward the door.

The woman's arm swung down like a gate, a smile pasted to her face. "Why the hurry?"

A sweet-and-sour stench hit me in the face. It seemed to be coming right through her skin. I thought about the bottles of alcohol Zoe had confiscated in the kitchen.

"She has to babysit, and I have to make dinner." Zoe hoisted her mom's arm up, giving us room to wiggle under. At the end of the hallway, she said, "Mom goes drinking with the girls once a week. They get kind of sloshed every now and then."

I gave her a sympathetic smile. I was halfway out the door when she jerked me back and threw her arms around me, crushing me in a bear hug. Caught off guard, I let go after a few seconds, but she held on tight.

"Don't tell Kade this, but I'm glad I joined the League. It's a nice diversion from real life," she said.

"I know what you mean." For the first time, I looked at Zoe and saw a potential friend.

She pulled back. "I've got to go now. I'm really the one with the babysitting job."

With an apologetic glance, she closed the door between us.

♪ CHAPTER 13 ♪

AS I SAT IN KADE'S APARTMENT, I WONDERED WHAT IT WAS like to live mostly on your own, without a mother around to nag you about picking up your junk. Did Kade's uncle even know he had visitors?

As Kade and Richie threw together snacks in the kitchen, I peeked into the hamper by the bathroom door. Sure enough, not only were his clothes in there, they weren't inside out. My own dirty clothes seemed to land everywhere but the hamper.

Over in the lone chair beside the window, Zoe flipped through magazines. When she went to use the bathroom, she left them in a pile on the floor. Within seconds Kade swooped down and returned them to the bookshelf.

Nora was the last to arrive. Apparently she wasn't used to doing her homework as fast as the rest of us. Kicking off her shoes, she plopped down in the middle of Kade's bed. Zoe and

Richie joined her. Personally, I didn't want to sit where Kade slept—and did who knows what else. But the only other choice was the floor. So I parked myself on the edge of the bed and leaned forward like a sprinter waiting for the starting gun.

Kade brought over a plate of homemade heart-shaped cookies. He circled the bed like a buzzard eyeing his prey, then descended beside me. The hairs on my arms tingled. I reached for a cookie before the sparks set off an explosion.

"Happy Valentine's Day," he said.

I'd forgotten all about it. No reason to remember. Mom and Dad hadn't mentioned it, maybe because they didn't want to draw attention to my seriously deficient social life. Or so they thought. I looked around the room at my new friends, my eyes lingering on Kade, the best Valentine's Day treat I'd had in a long time.

"They fixed the window in the back of the school," Richie reported. "All ground-level ones have new locks."

"That was fast," Zoe said.

"I think we should stay away from the school," Nora said. "Finish our plans somewhere else."

"Good point." Kade tapped her on the ankle, then left his hand beside her foot. I forced myself to look away. "For now, future plans will take place somewhere else."

I hated the way he looked at Nora. Beyond her eyes, into her, like he understood everything about her.

Kade hooked his elbow around Richie's neck. "This is your night, my friend. Dave Harper's next."

Richie's eyes widened. "For real?"

I heard someone exhale. Was Zoe disappointed that it wasn't her turn?

"Any ideas?" Kade asked.

"Maybe we could steal his clothes during practice," Nora offered.

"Are they practicing right now?" I asked.

"Yeah," Kade said. "Dave and those jocks are obsessed."

"What if we take their uniforms before they hit the field?" Richie said. "That would be hilarious."

Richie Morris had simple needs. That would be enough for him. But Kade said, "Think bigger."

"Maybe it should be more like a natural consequence," I said. My parents liked to throw that term around. It annoyed me to hear it on my own lips, but it did seem to fit the situation.

Kade raised an eyebrow. "Tell me more, Charlie."

The heat of his gaze melted my thoughts into a puddle. I struggled to re-form them. "Oh, um, well, it seems the reason he picked on Richie in the first place was . . ." I didn't know how to say it.

Kade helped. "Because he's gay. And?"

"So, maybe we could put a dent in Dave's lady-killer reputation."

Had I just said that? Was it really *me* coming up with the plan?

Before I could freak out at having an alter ego, Kade smiled. My reward.

"You'd better be in a different *country* when this happens," Nora warned Richie. "The first person Dave will point to is you."

Richie turned to Kade, panic flashing in his eyes. I figured he was upset about being on the receiving end of Dave's potential wrath, but Kade answered, "Don't worry. We'll find a good hiding spot. I won't let you miss this."

Richie broke into a grin.

For the next half hour, we refined the second revenge plot.

"How's this sound?" Nora asked. She held up a letter. "Hey, Dave—"

"His friends call him Big D," Richie interjected.

"Hey, Big D," Nora corrected. "I couldn't stop thinking about you all day. What happened between us was incredible. It was my first time. I know I'm not experienced, but I hope it was still good for you. I'll see you at nine tonight at the post office parking lot . . ."

"Put in 'like we talked about,'" Kade said. "The people who get this letter aren't going to show it to Dave. They have to think that he knows to show up."

I was impressed. Kade, the master of details. It was a good thing he wasn't a criminal, because he had a real mind for this stuff.

"Got it," Nora said. "So now it goes, 'I'll see you at nine tonight at the post office parking lot, like we talked about. Wear black. Until then, Michael.'"

"Did you put tomorrow's date on it?" Zoe asked.

"Of course," Nora said.

Because Dave Harper didn't know my voice, I was nominated to perform the next part. I wasn't sure I could pull off the seductive act, but here was my chance to show Kade a more enticing side of me.

"What about Caller ID?" asked Zoe.

"I'm unlisted," Kade said. "Comes up as 'Unknown.'"

My finger trembled as I punched in the number from the school directory.

"Hello?" He sounded half asleep.

"Hi," I whispered. "Is this Dave?"

"Yeah, who's this?"

"If you'd like to know, you'll have to meet me in the parking lot behind the post office at nine tomorrow night." I tried not to laugh. It was all so corny. Not to mention embarrassing.

"Oh, and wear black," I added.

"Why?" he asked.

"Why?" I mouthed to Nora.

She rolled her eyes and whispered: "No one can see what you're doing in the dark!"

"So no one can see what we're doing in the dark," I told him.

Nora pressed her mouth against Kade's chest, stifling a laugh. I stared at her, hoping she'd pull away, but she just turned her head, avoiding my eyes.

"Come on, who the hell is this? Don't jerk me around," Dave said.

Nora handed me page two of the script.

"It's time for us to meet. Believe me, you won't be disappointed . . ."

"Is this Ashley?"

"I'll see you tomorrow. I can't wait." I threw the phone down. True to form, I was blushing clear down to my toenails.

Kade leaned over, whispering into my ear, "I'd come running if I were him."

I turned my head so he wouldn't see that I was redder than a Hawaiian sunset. But then I saw the time on his alarm clock. *Crap.* "I told my parents I'd only be gone an hour. I have to go."

The way they stared at me, you'd think I'd just announced that aliens had landed in Glenwood.

"Do you always do everything they want?" Kade asked. The question was softened by the concern in his voice.

I looked down, not sure how to answer.

"Bye, Charlotte, see you next time." Nora dismissed me with a wave.

"This was really fun, thanks." I tacked on a smile for good measure.

Kade offered to walk me out. I pulled on my Keds and headed for the door. When we reached the stairs, he said, "I'm really glad you joined the League, Charlie."

All I could do was nod.

"Does anyone know the maximum value of the function?" Mr. Furino inquired, his voice weaving in and out of my thoughts.

It was eleven in the morning. Showtime. I put my head on the desk and imagined the "plan" in action.

"I need a bathroom pass," Zoe would moan to her study hall teacher. Then she'd sprint to the gymnasium, where she'd take a sip from the water fountain. Kade would move past her, into the boys' locker room. If anyone walked up, Zoe would have a coughing fit—Kade's sign to crawl into a shower stall until all was clear. But more than likely, he'd have time to insert the love letter through the vents in Mark Lawrence's locker. Later, probably at practice, Lawrence would open his locker and find the "misplaced" note addressed to "Big D."

Kade said he knew how these guys worked, that they'd come up with a plan to catch Dave in a compromising position. There was no lost love between Mark Lawrence and Dave Harper, Kade told us. Apparently, the coach had picked Dave, a lowly junior, as quarterback over Mark, a senior. Since then, Mark had been out to get the school superstar. I hadn't known any of this, but I wasn't exactly up on jock gossip. Kade, on the other hand, seemed to have his finger on the pulse of every living organism at Kennedy High.

I watched Mr. Furino explain the homework without hearing a word of it. When he turned to the board, my eyes swung back to the clock. Kade should've left the locker room, crossing paths with Zoe before they headed in opposite directions.

When the bell finally rang, I dashed out of the room and down the hall, looking for anyone who could tell me anything.

"Charlotte?"

I turned around, but it was only my orchestra stand partner, Amie.

"Hi," I said cheerfully, determined not to show my disappointment. It wasn't her fault that she wasn't one of us.

"Hey, Charlotte. Listen, I was wondering if you'd have time

after school to help me with the Mussorgsky. I get totally lost in the middle, and you can do it in your sleep."

"Oh, yeah, sure." I hadn't looked at the Mussorgsky in days. In fact, I hadn't touched my viola in the past forty-eight hours. A world record. But there was so much going on, what with the plans and my new friends. I briefly considered the homework that I was blowing off now that I actually had a life.

"I'm kind of busy at the moment," I told Amie. "Maybe next week?"

Her smile dimmed. "Oh, yeah, sure. That would work. Anytime."

With a wave, she disappeared into the science lab. I felt a pang of guilt but quickly dismissed it. Kade said guilt was for the weak-minded who couldn't stand behind their own actions.

My gaze moved like a pendulum, to the left, to the right, then up and down the stairs. It looked like I'd have to wait longer to get the details of part one.

As it turned out, it wasn't until after school, when I unfolded the paper airplane that had been flown through the bars of my instrument locker. One word, all in caps, scrawled diagonally across the back of a flyer for a youth leadership club: SUCCESS!

I let out a tiny squeal and allowed myself a smile that stayed on my face all the way home.

♪ CHAPTER 14 ♩

NOW WE JUST HAD TO WAIT FOR DAVE HARPER TO SHOW UP at the post office parking lot. We decided to meet thirty minutes early so we could find the best place to watch the scene unfold.

I hadn't counted on my parents getting in the way. Mom thinks that dinner is a sacred time, which wouldn't have mattered if it weren't for the fact that Dad came home an hour late.

"Maybe I should fire my client. The man never stops talking." He pitched his briefcase onto the recliner. "Even the three-hundred-dollar-an-hour fee doesn't shut him up. Sorry I'm late. What's for dinner?"

When he eyed the plates, forks, and knives arranged on the dining room table, I recognized my mistake. I'd never set the table in my life without the requisite lecture on teamwork and family. But today was different. I had somewhere to be.

"Let's eat," I said. "I'm starving."

Dad glanced at the table, then at me. "Looks nice."

"I didn't even have to nag," Mom said.

"I knew you'd be hungry when you got home, Dad."

Mom spooned corned beef onto our plates. My parents complained about the high heat bill. I dug in, eyeing the clock.

"How was school?" Mom asked.

The conversation was so . . . Disney. I had an urge to be honest, to poke holes in the family armor. *I'm going to sneak out with my friends, Mom and Dad. We're going to do something bad, and you can't stop me.*

The word "bad" stuck in my mind, bold as a marquee. I filed the image away. "Uh-huh," I said.

The forkful of limp cabbage paused halfway to Mom's mouth.

"Oh, fine, nothing new to report," I corrected.

Dad winked. "Same old, same old, huh?"

"Right."

Another fifty seconds were gone. What if I ran into Dave Harper on the way to the post office? Kade would be furious.

"So Charlotte, I have something to run by you," Dad began.

Oh God, not now! Dad's favorite dinner activity was to explain a case he'd been working on, then see how fast I could figure out a solution to his legal problem. If I got it right, he thumped me on the back. If I got it wrong, he lectured me on my fallible strategy. I was correct about 75 percent of the time, which Dad says is impressive, given my lack of training. But the thought of stumbling through a maze of legalities at that very moment made me want to vomit.

"My client hit a child with his car last year. He broke the boy's leg in six places. The small-time police department botched the job and didn't give him a Breathalyzer. He ended up walking, which irked a few hundred residents. Fast-forward two months. This same guy passes out in a stolen BMW, wrapping it around a utility pole. Here's the question: Can he get a fair trial within a hundred miles of his hometown?"

"Unlikely." I glanced at the clock and watched the second hand march forward. "The trial should be moved to a neighboring county to prevent juror prejudice."

Excellent, Charlie. I mean, Charlotte. That was a good, succinct answer!

"But what about—?"

I cut him off. "Dad, I'm feeling kind of tired. Think we can talk tomorrow?"

He raked his fingers through his thinning hair, leaving neat little rows of scalp. "I suppose it will still be an issue tomorrow."

Mom started clearing the dishes. "Why don't you go to bed, Charlotte? Make it an early night."

"Great idea." I dragged myself up the stairs.

Behind me, I heard Dad say, "What was that all about?"

Up in my bedroom, I tried to figure out a way to get out of the house. But I'd just told them I was tired, and it was a Monday evening—not a likely time for a spontaneous calculus tutoring session.

As hard as it was to do, I lay down in bed and waited. Mom would either show up to do a last-second check, or I'd be free to make my escape. A minute later, I had my answer.

"Do you need anything?" she asked, opening my door a crack. I kept my eyes and mouth shut. She pecked me on the forehead, no doubt checking for a fever.

"Sleep tight," she whispered.

I waited.

"Don't let the bedbugs bite," she added. Like always.

She shuffled out of my room in the slippers I gave her for Mother's Day a few years ago that were a size too big and would fall off her feet if she walked like a normal person. I heard the almost soundless shutting of my door.

Thirty seconds later, I stepped back to admire the lifelike "body" under my blanket. I was getting good at sneaking out. Some accomplishment.

I locked my bedroom door and carefully slid open the door to my porch. A minute later, I was scrambling up the side yard and sprinting down Maple Street.

Fluffy snowflakes drifted through the air as I raced into the post office parking lot. Kade, Richie, Zoe, and Nora hunkered down behind a blue sedan with multiple parking tickets stuck to the windshield.

"Looks like you could use some defrosting." Kade curled an arm around my waist. I moved in closer.

"We were wondering if you were going to show up," Nora said.

What was that supposed to mean? So I was a little late. She'd been late before, too.

"Sorry, I had a *huge* test to study for," I said, staring her down.

Kade and I huddled together, watching the snow swirl overhead. The flakes settled in his hair. Nora inserted a hand between us to brush them away. Kade didn't even flinch.

"You aren't easy to startle, are you?" I said.

"You're not the first one to say that."

Nora squinted at the dull numbers on her glow-in-the dark solar watch. "What if they don't show? How long do we plan to freeze our asses off?"

Zoe unwrapped three pieces of gum and popped them into her mouth. "Believe me, they'll show." She blew a bubble. "A jerk like Harper wouldn't miss the chance to have sex with—"

"Over there!" Richie pointed to a streetlamp in the corner of the parking lot.

I peered through the filthy sedan windows at Dave Harper, who stood under a flickering lamplight. He wore jeans with premade holes in the knees: required uniform among Kennedy High's elite.

I remembered begging Mom for a pair earlier in the year. They seemed like a ticket to the private world of high school cliques. Of course, my mother refused to shell out money for something she'd normally throw in the trash. But later in the day, I found her on the couch, methodically distressing my "back-to-school" jeans with a pair of sewing scissors.

Dave was only fifty feet away. As my eyes traced the slope of arm muscles beneath his football jersey, Zoe adjusted her position, accidentally stepping on a full bag of potato chips that someone had abandoned. It made an explosive popping noise— or at least it seemed that way, accentuated by my nerves. Dave's head snapped in our direction. He reached up, twisting the brim of his baseball cap to the back.

"Who's there?" he called out.

I held my breath. Snowflakes tapped on the dry leaves. Dave paced over to a postal truck, checked his reflection in the side mirror, and walked back. He shoved his hands into his pockets, shifting his weight from foot to foot. He wouldn't wait around much longer.

Just then, Mark Lawrence and his crew came into view, hopping like Mexican jumping beans from the grocery store toward the lot. The five of us were like spectators at Wimbledon, our heads swiveling back and forth from Harper to Lawrence.

"Hey, who's there?" Dave squinted into the night.

"It's Mikey," crooned Mark. "Your boooooyfriend."

I don't know why, but all along, I'd pictured Mark hiding behind the building, waiting to see if Dave would show up. Then he'd sneak off and tell the entire school. But this was heading in a different direction. I dried my sweaty palms on my scarf.

"What are you talking about?" Dave asked. "Mikey who?"

Mark emerged from the shadows. His buffoons surrounded Dave in seconds.

"Why are you here, Mark?" Dave asked.

"Did Mikey-baby stand you up?"

Dave delivered the classic smile that seemed to dissolve most of Kennedy's female population. "Look, guys, I have no clue what's going on here. This is some kind of joke, right?"

"Ha, ha, ha." Mark tossed Nora's balled-up note in Dave's face. "Your little fairy friend put this in the wrong locker."

I winced at the derogatory term and glanced at Richie. He was enjoying the show, the smallest of smiles tugging at his mouth.

Dave smoothed out the note, and holding it under a ray of light, read it. He let it slip through his fingers. It fell into a puddle where it floated on the surface like a paper boat. "Come on, man. You've known me for three years. I've slept with every girl at Kennedy High."

"Talk about an inflated sense of self-worth," Nora whispered.

Mark's fist shot out, connecting with Dave's jaw. Dave fell to the ground, his baseball hat skidding across the blacktop.

"Jesus, Lawrence, what the hell's the matter with you?"

"I don't like pansies, that's what's the matter!" Mark yelled.

Dave scrambled backward like a crab, carried by his hands and feet. "I told you, I'm no—"

The pack descended, pounding at Dave's legs. One of the guys delivered a kick to his stomach. Dave contracted into a ball, groaning. This wasn't how it was supposed to go. He was supposed to walk away humiliated, not pummeled. Weren't jocks supposed to have a team-for-life mentality?

I covered my eyes, but I couldn't block out Dave's grunts and moans as the others took turns punching and kicking the exposed parts of his body.

I peeked at Kade though my fingers. Shadows from a nearby tree cut his face in half.

"This wasn't supposed to happen," I whispered to him. "We have to do something."

My eyes pulled back to Dave. He wiped his nose, leaving a bloody trail along his shirtsleeve. "Is this about football?" he cried, rolling onto his knees. "'Cause it's just a game, Lawrence, a damn game."

Lawrence lunged forward, shoving Dave down again. I heard the sickening crack of bone as Dave's arm collapsed under his weight. He howled and drew it to his chest.

I grabbed Kade's shirt. "We have to stop this," I pleaded. "It's getting out of control."

"No, it's just getting good," he whispered. He put a finger to his lips while keeping his eyes on the horrible scene before us. "Quiet, Charlie."

"You broke it!" Dave cried, stumbling to his feet. "Jesus Christ, you broke my goddamned arm!"

Lawrence actually looked shocked, his eyes widening as he took a step closer to check it out. That's when Dave made his move, driving the elbow of his good arm into Lawrence's gut. His teammate doubled over, and Dave took off. Just like in football, no matter how injured these guys were, they could still gain yardage. Fistfuls of rocks flew over Dave's head as he vanished down an alley.

"Oh my God," I said, watching Mark and his friends slap each other's hands as they crossed the parking lot. "Do you think he'll be OK?"

Kade grabbed my arm. "It's time to get out of here."

"Too bad he got away," Nora said. "He deserved it."

I stared at her. Was this the same girl who saw a B as failure, who'd spent her whole life trying to please others?

Kade's viselike grip hurt my arm. "Relax, Charlie. Nora's right."

Once the guys had left, Kade jogged over to the blacktop, scooped something up, and stuffed it into his pocket. Then he turned around, both thumbs raised. Nora, Richie, and Zoe returned the gesture.

I stared beyond Nora's head, watching Dave in my memory, curled up to protect himself against the attack.

"Think of what he did to Richie," Nora said. "Now he knows what it feels like."

I could see what she was saying: Dave had experienced for himself what it felt like to be harassed. But the irony didn't slip by me. Now I knew what it felt like to be a bully, too.

They all turned to me, waiting. Kade wrinkled his nose as if he could sniff my hesitation. I shook my head, trying to clear my thoughts, which were as sticky and thick as tar. He said something, but I couldn't hear him from that distance. All I could focus on was his mouth, slightly open, and his eyebrows, arched with an unspoken question.

I hesitated, then lifted my thumb.

♪ CHAPTER 15 ♪

SINCE ZOE LIVED TWO BLOCKS FROM THE POST OFFICE, and her mom worked Monday nights, Kade picked her house to celebrate what Nora was calling "Harper's Ass-Kicking Party."

The stench of trash wafted through the door before it was opened. A pair of flies buzzed over something left in a bowl on the arm of a recliner.

Kade couldn't deal with the mess. He sunk to the sofa and started channel surfing while Richie and Nora picked through a bag of stale corn chips.

"You don't think Mr. Reid will connect the gym office with Dave Harper getting beat up, do you?" I asked.

"How?" Kade said. "Who's going to tell him?"

"If Mark or Dave talk, he might figure out that someone planted the letter."

"They won't," Kade said, as if he'd received the answer from his personal crystal ball. "Teammates support each other. Jock superglue. Dave won't rat on his defensive lineman, and Mark won't admit that he beat up the star quarterback."

It sounded reasonable. Nora, Richie, and Zoe nodded.

In her mom's bedroom, Zoe flattened down onto her stomach and shimmied under the bed, exiting out the other side with a Costco box full of liquor bottles.

Nora reached for the whiskey, raising it in the air. "I'd like to make a toast. To being wild, crazy, and free."

Zoe snatched it out of Nora's hand. "That's a six-dollar drugstore special. Here, try this." She handed Nora a skinny, square bottle. "It's the only one I'll touch."

Nora took a hearty swig. She reminded me of a fault line, shifting and straining all the time. "My favorite part was seeing Harper on his knees, begging Lawrence not to beat him to a pulp," she said, wiping her mouth with the back of her hand.

I sensed Zoe's eyes on me. I knew I was being too quiet, but images of Harper cowering on the cement kept playing through my head. Zoe leaned across Nora and offered the bottle to me. Was this a test? I raised it to my lips and swallowed. My eyes watered as the liquid burned a trail down my throat.

Zoe slapped me on the back. "Want some water?"

Kade scooped my foot into his lap. All my brainpower sunk into the pinkie toe he was massaging.

"This is where you hold your tension," he said.

"That tickles!" I giggled, drawing my feet under me.

He moved closer. "Hmm. This could be fun."

"Get a room," Nora snapped.

I looked to Kade for my defense, but he was lost in thought, stroking the stubble above his lip.

♪ CHAPTER 16 ♪

I'M A PASSENGER IN A HELICOPTER, AND WE'RE FLYING over the rain forest. Kade, the pilot, throws me an easy smile over his shoulder.

All of a sudden, the craft lurches. Kade adjusts the controls, correcting the trajectory.

"Poor Charlie. You have a problem with trust," he says as we soar above the treetops.

But then the chopper plunges into a downward spiral. I look at Kade. He doesn't seem at all concerned that we're about to crash. His gaze remains fixed on the windshield.

"Do you even know how to fly this thing?" I yell above the dying groans of the engine.

I look out the window and see the earth getting closer. I squeeze my eyes shut, seconds before the helicopter slams into the ground and splinters into hundreds of pieces.

• • •

I woke with a start, terror pulsing through my body. It's not real, I told myself. Just a dream. Just a dream. Just a dream. I repeated the words until I fell asleep again.

"Do you suffer from blemish overload?" inquired a squeaky-voiced teen. "Do pimples get in the way of your good times? Then zap those zits with—"

I fumbled for the cord to my radio alarm clock, yanking it from the wall.

The next thing I knew, Mom was tapping me on the back. "Charlotte, it's almost seven!"

The details of last night slammed into me with alarming clarity, officially waking me up. "I'm sick," I told her. My eyelashes felt stuck together.

She laid her cool hand across my forehead. "Not even warm. Get up."

"Haven't you heard of a mental-health day?"

"No. What's that?"

"It's when kids need a break from school to gather strength so they can make it through senior year."

She smiled. "You can't run from your problems, sweetheart."

Running? Who was running? I was jogging in place.

My conversation with Mom made me fifteen minutes late for class—my third tardy in two weeks. At least I had a note from home, saving me from detention. The hallways were empty, so I slowed down and took the long way to class.

I tensed when I saw Nora's PE teacher by the door of the

teachers' lounge, gripping a thick white mug with permanent coffee stains. Mascara tears rolled down her face and dripped onto the collar of her cream blouse. I froze, paralyzed by the sight. I'd never seen a teacher cry before. It seemed so . . . out of place.

Mrs. Wilkerson, the art teacher, stood beside Madame Detroit. I ducked into the girls' bathroom and cupped my ear to the swinging door.

"I was only going to be a substitute until Marsha recovered." Madame's accent was faint, hardly noticeable. Unlike Nora's impersonation.

"I have to admit, Pauline, I'm worried. What message will it send?"

"I tried to deal with it. But I can't imagine who would hate me enough to do this," she said. "These are angry kids. I can't help but wonder what they'll do next. All I know is I don't want to be around to find out."

"The police think it's a senior prank," Wilkerson said.

I let out my breath. Finally, someone got it.

"I suppose Tutti's some kind of joke, too?"

Tutti? What was she talking about? My orchestra teacher, still recovering from her breakdown, hadn't returned to school yet.

"I know it's—" Wilkerson's voice faded.

I nudged the door open and leaned closer. Without warning, it swung inward, smacking me in the face. I stepped back, stunned. Samantha Hawkins glanced at me with mild curiosity and headed for a stall. Over the sound of peeing, she called out, "There are easier ways to get a new nose."

I pushed the door open and sped past the teachers, holding my sore nose. I could feel their eyes on my back. Lucky for me, I'd shown zero talent in introduction to charcoal drawing last semester. My name wouldn't survive Wilkerson's short-term memory.

During the break between third and fourth period, I slipped notes into my fellow League members' lockers, asking them to meet me in a music practice room after school. With its soundproof walls and thick curtains, it was the perfect place to hold an emergency meeting.

Kade was the last to arrive, Richie in tow. "I hope this is important," he said, pulling the already-drawn curtain a quarter inch to the left. He shrugged off his backpack. It dropped to the floor like a lead weight.

I looked at him, taken aback by his attitude.

Richie sent me an apologetic glance. "Reid was following us again, but we lost him in the crowd."

"What do you mean?" I asked. I remembered what Richie had said about how Mr. Reid watched them sometimes. But following them around was a lot creepier.

"Does he know something about . . . ?" Nora glanced at the closed curtain but lowered her voice, anyway. "Well, you know. Us."

"Nah, this is nothing new. He's been stalking Richie and me for a long time. Before the League," Kade said.

Richie dropped his chin to his chest. "He hates me. Kade says he won't let up until I leave the school . . . or graduate, if I last that long."

"If you go, I go. We're a unit," Kade said. Richie looked up, a smile spreading across his face.

"Why is he following you? Because of the drug thing?" I asked. I still couldn't see why Mr. Reid would care one way or the other about Richie's private life.

"I told you, he's a homophobic bastard," Kade erupted. "Anyway, I don't want to talk about that asshole. What's up, Charlie? Why are we here? I'm the one who calls the League meetings."

I lowered my head like a wounded puppy. "Madame's quitting," I whispered.

Nora let out a victorious whoop, which, thankfully, was swallowed by the acoustic foam tiles. Was I the only one who felt guilty that Kennedy High was losing a teacher?

As Kade looked at me, the bearer of good news, a genuine smile replaced the frown that had been etched into his face a moment earlier. "Well, I guess that's a good enough reason, Charlie."

I was glad I had a sweater on, because it covered up the goose bumps that sprung into action when he directed his topaz eyes in my direction.

"What's with you?" Zoe whispered in my ear. "Your neck is all red."

"Um, allergic to cafeteria food," I mumbled.

Zoe started to tell a joke she'd heard, but I phased out, my thoughts returning to Madame. Why didn't it bother them? We'd done more than send a message; we'd made a teacher quit. And she was leaving because she was afraid. Afraid of us.

Richie laughed at the punch line. I did, too, but only because Kade's eyes were like radar, scanning the horizon for blips on the screen.

"I've got a better one." Richie turned to Kade. "You tell it. The Adam and Eve joke."

Kade laughed. "You know how it goes."

"No one tells it like you," Richie said.

They shared an unreadable look, then Kade glanced away. A second later, he looked back, holding Richie's gaze. Richie blinked and lowered his eyes. It was disconcerting, their exchange. Something I couldn't, or didn't want, to define. I checked Richie's ears. Sure enough, they were red.

"Oh, wait, I think I know that one," Nora shrieked. "Let me tell it!"

Kade waved Nora on. She rewound the joke to get it right. Kade leaned back in his chair, observing us with pride as if we were everything he'd ever hoped for. His royal court.

"You feeling OK, Charlotte?" Richie asked.

I nodded, thinking about my AP history class last semester when Mr. Rickman read a quote aloud from the first Inaugural Address of Franklin D. Roosevelt, thirty-second president of the United States: "The only thing we have to fear is fear itself."

"Sure," I told them. "Everything's great."

♪ CHAPTER 17 ♫

TIFFANY MILLER'S NEWEST BOYFRIEND, A SCRAGGLY HAIRED foreign-exchange student from Paris, pressed her to the cafeteria wall, devouring her with a gaping, hungry mouth. Every few seconds, Tiffany stepped back to get some air. Of course, the public act of lust was for the benefit of the student body. Tiffany was the Most Desired Female at Kennedy, and everyone had to know it. I hoped she'd faint from oxygen deprivation.

I spotted Zoe, sitting alone at a table by the arched entrance to the cafeteria. She also watched Tiffany, who made a halfhearted attempt to slip out of her boyfriend's grip. The struggle seemed to turn him on more. Free at last, Tiffany glided through the cafeteria like a bride at a reception, garnering more votes for prom queen.

Zoe caught my eye. She strutted to the snack line, imitating Tiffany's Barbizon-graduate walk. It looked like she was modeling the latest in Third Infantry Division wear. I laughed into my napkin.

When lunch was over, I followed Tiffany and Monsieur Paris as they stumbled down the hall, occasionally veering to the side to let people pass. I turned toward the locker beside me and pretended it was mine. It didn't matter, though; they didn't know I was alive. Monsieur Paris's hand swept under Tiffany's shirt, and she tossed her head back, laughing.

With a seductive smile, he strutted off. Tiffany waited for him to turn a corner, then walked past me into her classroom. A few years ago, she would've elbowed me as she passed by, but now I'd turned invisible. I could live with that.

I stood there, thinking of Kade—imagining his lips, a velvet softness, seeking mine . . .

"Miss Brody? The bell is for class. Not naptime." My calculus teacher, Mr. Furino, stood in front of me, wearing his lunchtime workout gear. I clutched my backpack to my stomach and moved past him.

A crash of something hard against metal snapped me out of my lust-induced daze.

"What's going on?" asked Jill Bengley from behind me.

"Morris is getting the crap beaten out of him," someone answered.

Another voice said, "It was only a matter of time before he got his butt kicked."

A book slid out of my arms. I didn't bother to pick it up. I tore around the corner, crashing into kids.

Beside the stairs, Richie was crumpled on the floor, his shoulders trembling with quiet sobs. Blood trickled down his chin.

Dave Harper stood over him. "I know you're behind this. You were at the post office, weren't you? I know I heard someone back there." He bent down, giving Richie a magnified view of his arm cast. "Doc says no sports for months. How about I break both your legs as payback?"

Richie closed his eyes.

"Lost your voice, homo? Whatcha think?" Dave gave him a shove with his uninjured arm. Richie rolled onto his side, retracting his legs to his chest like a turtle without a shell.

I couldn't stand it any longer. I'd only taken one step when someone grabbed my shirt and yanked me back. I jerked around, fists clenched.

Kade's eyes were slits. "It's under control, Charlie."

His grip on my wrist was so tight that the slightest movement hurt. I glanced at Richie, helpless. "But we can't just let him—"

Kade's other hand clamped over my mouth. I had a sudden urge to sink my teeth into his palm. How could he stand by and let his best friend get pummeled? What was wrong with him?

"Get the hell out of my way!" cried a familiar voice.

Zoe barreled through the crowd, pushing people to the side like bowling pins. I waited for Kade to charge her, but he stayed still and slowly lowered his hand from my mouth.

Zoe wedged herself between Dave and Richie. "Get away from him!" she cried.

Dave grinned. "Oh, look at this, a girl's come to your defense."

I couldn't stand there and watch Zoe get slammed. I shook

my arm free of Kade's grip and lunged forward, but he snagged my shirt again and reeled me back.

"Stop it," I said. "They need us!"

"Back off!" Zoe cried, giving Dave a shove. She kneeled down.

"Who the hell are you?" Dave asked.

"His girlfriend, that's who."

That's when I got it: this was a performance, written and directed by Kade Harlin.

Zoe twirled her fingers through Richie's hair. "Are you OK, baby?"

Dave shook his head and laughed. "You've got to be kidding. Gay boy has a girlfriend? Yeah, whatever."

"I don't care what you believe, douchebag." Zoe jumped to her feet, her nose an inch from Dave's.

"You want to tell me where lover boy was Monday night?" His voice was as hard as the fist by his side.

"Which Monday?" Zoe asked innocently.

"Four days ago," Dave said. He looked down at Richie. "I think you know which Monday, loser."

"That's an easy one. He was at my house." She lifted her T-shirt, which read SUPPORT OUR TROOPS, and leaned over to wipe a spot of blood off Richie's chin. Everyone gawked at her black lace bra. "All night," she added.

Zoe leaned down to kiss Richie on the mouth, then stood up and turned on the heel of her boot.

Dave slipped into the crowd.

Zoe reached behind her back for Richie's hand and dragged him down the hallway behind her.

The show was over. Everyone scattered to class. All except Kade. I counted the stains on the frayed tan carpet.

"Richie's my best friend," Kade said. "You think I was going to let him get the crap beaten out of him? I knew this would happen, Charlotte. I had a plan."

Not Charlie. *Charlotte.*

"I'm sorry," I said, rubbing the dull throb in my wrist.

Slowly, like the sun climbing above the horizon, he smiled. The whiteness of his teeth brightened the dimly lit hallway.

"Forgiven," he said, caressing the tip of my chin.

♪ CHAPTER 18 ♫

RICHIE, ZOE, AND I CAUGHT UP WITH EACH OTHER THREE blocks from school.

"How are you doing?" I asked him.

He tried to smile, despite a lip that was double in size. "Never better."

Zoe raised her right hand. "So, Morris, you promise to tell the whole truth and nothing but the truth?"

"Scout's honor," he said. "Never mind. Scratch that, the scouts hate gays."

"Did you feel anything when I kissed you this afternoon? Even the tiniest anything?"

Richie scratched his head. "Uh, you mean like fireworks?"

"Yeah, yeah, yeah."

"It was as exciting as . . . flossing a piece of spinach from my teeth."

Zoe swung a notebook at him. It made contact with his hip,

and he flinched. "I bet I did wonders for your image," she said.

"I don't care what anyone thinks of me!" he bristled.

Zoe stuck her tongue out at his mini-outburst. "Just joking, my friend."

Personally, I was relieved to catch a glimpse of his backbone. Richie muttered an apology and bent down to tie shoelaces that were already double-knotted.

Zoe shook her head dramatically. "Richie Morris, I hereby declare that you're undeniably, irreversibly . . ."

"Contentedly . . . ," I added.

"Gay!" we said together, cracking up.

We fell onto the damp, semi-frozen grass next to the sidewalk. I wrapped my scarf around my mouth, closed my eyes, and tried to soak in the weak rays of sunlight.

"Yo, Morris!"

My eyes flew open. Dave Harper loomed over us. I searched the street for Kade, willing him to pop up from behind a parked car. I'd come to believe that he was always around, somewhere. Contrary to my theory, he didn't surface.

I could throw myself at Dave's leg, I thought; that might buy time for Richie to run away. Then again, if a 250-pound defensive lineman couldn't stop the school quarterback, what prayer did I have?

"For the record, I don't get you, Morris," Dave said. "But I guess I misread you. So I'm apologizing, OK?"

He glanced at Zoe, his eyes drifting down.

"The right boob accepts your apology," Zoe said. "But the left one thinks you're an asshole."

Dave aimed his keys at an emerald green convertible parked down the street. It chirped twice. "Well, I've got business to do. No one's going to mess with me and get away with it."

He strode to his car, and with a screechy U-turn, sped away.

Zoe bowed. "Hear ye! Hear ye! The great Dave Harper has apologized. Sort of. Not for trying to kick your ass or anything, just for thinking you were—gasp—*gay*. Let's go find Kade. He won't believe this!"

Richie tensed. "No! Don't tell him."

Zoe pursed her lips but didn't say anything.

"Why? Dave thinks you're not involved," I said. "That should make Kade happy."

Richie rose to his feet, peeling a strand of wet grass off his pants. "I'll call him later. He doesn't want anyone to see us together. Not ever."

He swung his backpack onto his shoulders, gave a closed-mouthed smile, and walked away.

♪ CHAPTER 19 ♪

COLLEGE ADMISSIONS WERE ROLLING IN NOW, AND HOME-work had slowed to a crawl. The teachers probably assumed the seniors wouldn't do the work, anyway. Suddenly, I had a lot more time on my hands. Time to think. Time to worry.

I checked out a mystery from the library, but the first paragraph read like a continual loop, fading into the background of my fear. I heard the crunch of a postage meter against glass. I smelled the acrid plastic of a burning grade book. I saw myself in the parking lot, taking the punches and kicks for Dave Harper.

It had been two weeks since our revenge against the school quarterback. Kade thought we should lie low for a while before starting our next plan. He didn't want Reid connecting the dots, he said. That sounded great to me, but for a different reason. I needed a little time to settle down myself.

Images from the League's plans were flipping through my mind like a slide show. I wished I could talk to someone who might understand. But Kade had made it clear that we weren't to discuss the League with anyone.

Cleaning my room was my mother's prescription for boredom. So on Sunday afternoon, I divided my clothes into two piles—Dorky and Passable. As I threw away socks that hadn't seen their mates in years, I got lost in my favorite daydream.

I'm in Kade's apartment, but I can't find him.

"Here, Charlie!" he calls from the bathroom.

I open the door. He's standing under a surge of steaming spray. Skin, glistening with soapsuds. I move closer, one step, then another . . .

"Hello?" I picked up my ringing cell phone.

"Hi, Charlotte, it's Nora."

"Oh, hi." I fell back onto the bed.

"What are you doing?"

"Organizing my black hole of a bedroom."

"Wow, that sounds like fun. Listen, you want to come over? I was thinking of having a barbecue. My parents are at a wedding in Colorado. They told me no big parties, then they had the nerve to laugh at the idea. It's embarrassing how little they think of me."

I looked outside. "A winter barbecue?"

"No prob. We have a fire pit."

"Oh, OK. So, uh, who's coming?" I took a swig of Diet Coke, swishing it around like mouthwash.

Like, will Kade be there?

"Just you, me, and Richie. Zoe had an emergency. Her mom's boss called to say she puked all over the tomato display, and Zoe needs to pick her up."

I felt sorry for Zoe. She was always on call.

"What about Kade?" I asked.

"He has to check in with his probation officer, I think."

The carbonated soda, halfway down my throat, reversed direction. "Probation officer?"

"Something to do with an old shoplifting charge."

I pictured Kade stealing candy from a drugstore. Or maybe he'd robbed a warehouse in the middle of the night. It could go either way. Then I began to wonder why he'd share something so private with Nora, or more to the point, not with me? The serrated side of jealousy cut into me.

"He didn't tell me," I said.

She paused. "Why would he?"

I couldn't think of a response.

"So are you coming or not?" she asked.

I glanced at the hill of clothes in the Dorky pile. "I'll be right over."

With sky-blue siding and gingerbread trim, 23 Meadow Court looked more like a birthday cake than a residence. A flagstone path, embedded in an expanse of synthetic grass, parted the massive yard. It took almost a minute to walk to the door.

Richie invited me in with a bow and a flourish of the hand.

"Thanks, Jeeves." I laughed, following him up a winding stairwell.

Nora's bedroom was like a five-year-old's fantasy. The walls were cotton-candy pink, and an enormous canopy bed, complete with lavender bedding that matched the lace curtains, sat in the middle of the room like a centerpiece. An overweight teddy bear with a missing arm perched on a pillow.

I looked around. Nora wasn't there. "Who kidnapped the princess?"

"She's retrieving iced tea and crystal goblets for her royal guests," Richie said.

Honor Roll certificates, from the sixth grade up, wallpapered Nora's closet. Most were printed on pale-blue card stock, her name a shimmering swirl of calligraphy. *Principal's Honor Roll.*

"Maybe she can still be valedictorian," I said. "It was her dream."

"It wasn't a dream. It was a goal."

"What's the difference?" I traced my finger along the gold border of a certificate. It was as close to straight A's as I would get.

"A dream is a wish. A fantasy. It's based on luck more than skill," he said. "A goal's a measurable vision to achieve your dream. Believe me, I've spent way too long thinking about this."

Maybe my view of Richie as a parrot, echoing other people's words, wasn't exactly accurate. He probably had a lot of interesting thoughts that he silenced for whatever reason.

Nora swept into the room, balancing a pitcher of iced tea and three wineglasses on a shiny silver tray. "I know what you're thinking," she said. "It's my mother's fault. I asked her if I could paint the walls a different color. She practically hyperventilated."

She sat down at the window seat and poured the tea. When she caught my eye, I realized that my finger was still on the certificate. I dropped my hand to my side.

"I was a real Goody Two-shoes until I met you guys," she said.

"Now you're rotten like us," Richie responded.

"All the books, the studying . . ." She added a soapbox-preacher drawl. "Then along comes the League of Strays, and I'm reborn!"

"Hallelujah!" Richie cried.

We clinked our glasses together.

"Maybe we can lose the name now," I said. "We're just friends, right?"

"I don't know," Richie said. "About the name, I mean. Not the friends part."

"I'm not perfect, you know," Nora said, lost in her own tangential conversation. "But I'm perfect at pretending to be perfect."

Richie and I made a show of rolling our eyes.

"Open my closet if you don't believe me."

I slid the pocket door open, expecting to find her clothes arranged by type, season, and color. An avalanche of junk tumbled out.

"The true me is in that closet," Nora said.

"Don't worry," Richie told her, a solemn expression on his face. "I'm in the closet, too."

I did my best to cram all the stuff back inside. It didn't matter to me whether Nora was perfect or not, but I *was* curious why she invested so much time trying to appear that way.

"Thank God Kade set me straight," she said.

Richie looked away, pensive. "He's pretty amazing."

Nora jumped to her feet. "Hey, you guys want to see my sister's room?"

She didn't wait for an answer. Richie and I trailed behind her to the end of the hallway. Running a finger over the ledge of the door frame, she brought down a straightened paper clip and jabbed it into a hole in the doorknob.

The bedroom was a monument to a dead teenager. Pictures of Nora's sister smothered the wall. I moved in, studying a close-up of Kelly's leg in the air, soccer ball angling toward a goal post. In the photograph below it, she wore a strapless yellow cocktail dress. She barely reached the chest of the cute boy beside her. I didn't get it. What would possess someone like her to commit suicide?

From behind me, Nora said, "According to the autopsy report, she was ten weeks pregnant. My sister would rather OD on migraine medicine than tell my mother and father she was knocked up."

I wondered what it would feel like to tell my parents something like that. They'd freak out for a day or two, I was sure, and my mother would probably shed a few pounds in tears, but eventually we'd discuss what to do next. I knew they'd be there for me, no matter what.

"They could've helped her," I said.

"You don't know my parents." She removed a brass frame from the wall, polished it with the cuff of her shirt, then hung it back up. "When my sister died, they anointed her Saint Kelly. I've wasted too much time competing with an almighty ghost." Her eyes went glassy, threatening tears.

Richie handed her a faded box of tissues. They'd probably sat in that room, untouched, for the past five years. Nora waved it away. "Enough of my blabbering. So are we going to barbecue or what?"

Out in the yard, the sun wove in and out of pillowy clouds. The chilly breeze rocked the chimes dangling from the trellis. I set the table with a matching set of floral outdoor plates, napkins, and cups while Nora struggled to light the fire pit. Richie was in charge of the food, which was fine with me since scrambled eggs were the extent of my culinary repertoire.

"I think I'll stuff the hamburgers with feta cheese. Or maybe marinate them in a teriyaki sauce," he said, rinsing his hands in the built-in sink beside the grill.

I was impressed. "Where'd you learn to cook?"

"After my mom died, it was either that or eat at McDonald's every night."

He rattled off a list of his favorites. My mouth watered. Black bean lasagna, butternut squash casserole, and something called caramelized onion and goat cheese gratin. At chez Brody, my version of a gourmet meal consisted of a can of cream of chicken soup and a bag of frozen vegetables mixed with macaroni.

The grill sizzled, juices from the meat dripping onto the hot coals. Richie had never looked so relaxed, surrounded by ingredients and barbecue tools.

"I want to open a restaurant one day," he said so quietly I almost didn't hear him. "If I can convince people that it's not a dumb idea."

"It doesn't sound dumb," I said. "Where will it be?"

"On a cliff, overlooking the Caribbean Sea. Whenever the hungry locals knock on my door, I'll open for business."

"Maybe you can be his bartender," Nora said to me, moving to the lawn chair. She lifted her shirt to her bra line in a futile attempt to tan her stomach. "Can you believe we're almost done with high school?"

"I hope college is an improvement," Richie mumbled.

High school hadn't been a joy ride for me, either, but I knew it didn't compare to Richie's experience. I thought about Sam Burgess, my ninth-grade crush, and how I'd "coincidentally" run into him in front of his classroom every day. If Richie liked a guy and anyone found out, he'd get pummeled. My eyes skirted the bruise on his left arm. He already had.

"Should I text Zoe?" Nora asked, her eyes closed to the sun.

"She'll call if she wants to come over," I said. I didn't want to remind Zoe of what she was missing. It seemed her mom demanded a lot of attention these days.

Richie flipped the burgers. A puff of smoke spiraled into the air. "I can't believe I'm saying this, but I actually wish Zoe was here. I kind of like her blunt honesty. Crazy, huh?"

I knew what he meant. With Zoe, you didn't have to read between the lines.

"I don't get why she hangs out with us, frankly," Nora said. "She's done everything in her power to scare away friends."

I remembered the bear hug Zoe gave me when I was at her house that first time. "That's just a defense. She pushes people away so they won't get too close."

"It's not like she gets the opportunity to bring home play-dates," Richie said.

"She needs us," I told Nora. "And she definitely needs the escape."

"Whoa, we have a resident psychologist in our midst." Sarcasm bled through Nora's words. "Maybe Charlotte wants to give Kade a run for his money."

"I'm not Kade," I blurted out.

Nora shielded the sun with her hand, tilting her head back to look at me. "That was a compliment, *Charlie*."

I blushed. It was time to change the subject. "Have you told your dad that you're—"

"A fag?" Richie interrupted.

I tensed. "No, Richie. *Gay*. Don't use that other word."

"Everyone else says it."

"Well, you're not everyone."

He took in my humorless expression. "Yeah, my dad knows. I told him over the summer. He said he always knew. But my brother? Well, Tony's a different story."

Richie looked at the last corncob, over-roasted and rusty-orange. He rolled it onto his plate.

I poured some iced tea into his empty glass. "I'm sure he'll come around."

"Kade said it was too soon to tell him. I should've listened. Kade understands people."

"Too well," I said without thinking. I fixed a smile on my face to lighten the words.

"He's been my only friend since middle school."

"But now you've got us, too," I said.

"So what's it like being gay?" Nora leaned forward like a talk-show host trying to get the scoop.

"Um, well, for starters, I keep it to myself."

"How do you know you're gay? I mean, if you haven't actually . . . ?" I couldn't finish the sentence.

"What Charlotte means is, how do you know you're a homosexual if you haven't actually had *sex* with a guy?"

Richie's face turned the color of a fuchsia sweater hanging over the handle of my closet at home. "Um, that's not exactly true. It was at camp, last summer, in Yosemite. His name was Ray."

"Oh my God," Nora squealed. "How was it?"

Richie looked away, blushing. "I don't kiss and tell."

Nora traded questions like a seasoned reporter. "So what happened when camp was over? Did you see him again?"

Richie looked uncomfortable, the way I'd felt when Kade had made us share stories of our past humiliations. Like the one that never happened, said a voice in my head.

"I bet you're having a secret long-distance affair," she continued.

Richie poked at the dwindling stack of burgers. "I wrote him a letter when I got home. It took him a month to write back. A newsy letter, the kind you get from your grandma. He told me about this girl he'd met at his homecoming dance, thanked me for a fun time at summer camp, and that was that."

"Well, college is a whole different enchilada," Nora said.

Richie looked like he wanted to climb into the firepit. "Yeah, maybe." He sunk his teeth into the overdone corncob.

"This marinade's great, Richie," I said. "Soy sauce and mustard? I bet we'll have a lot of repeat customers at the Brody and Morris Cliffside Restaurant."

He pretended to be offended. "Oh, so now you're a partner, huh?" He sent me a lopsided smile of gratitude. Even so, I knew my help was about as effective as a Band-Aid on a broken leg.

♪ CHAPTER 20 ♪

MONDAY MORNING, MOM DECIDED TO STRENGTHEN OUR mother-daughter bond over a bowl of Cheerios.

"I know this was a rough move for you, Charlotte. I'm so happy you've adjusted to school." The smile didn't mask the concern in her eyes.

I looked down at the cut-up chunks of banana floating on top of my cereal. I hated bananas in Cheerios. Always had. Why didn't she know this?

"You can talk to me about anything," she said.

My mother was like the dishtowel in her hand, ready to soak up the details of my life. I wanted to talk to someone who would listen, but I wasn't *that* desperate.

"Mom, you need to get a life," I snapped.

Pure meanness didn't make me feel better. I wished I could take the words back. She swooped down on my half-eaten bowl of cereal and headed for the kitchen before I could apologize.

I picked up my instrument. "Everything's great, Mom. You don't have to worry."

I waited for her usual good-bye, with a perky "Have a nice day!" at the end, but all I heard was the rumble of the dishwasher.

My mother seemed to annoy me more every day, but it wasn't fair to react the way I had. Kade was right about my parents; they were too involved in my life. I hoped Mom would loosen her grip on me so I wouldn't have to shake her off.

In English, Mr. Holmquist pounced on me the nanosecond my eyes glazed over. *I'm a senior*, I wanted to say. *Go pick on a freshman for chrissakes.* Instead, I asked, "Um, what was the question again?"

"Would you please explain what the broken rose in chapter seven means?" he asked, tacking on a tired sigh.

Nothing, I thought. The author was describing her favorite flower as a kid, but meanwhile, in schools across America, people were finding the demise of communism in a bent stem.

I didn't think the answer would suffice, so I just blinked.

Mr. Holmquist turned his back to the class and scrawled the next day's homework on the whiteboard. I laid my head on my arms and watched the clock, desperate for the ten-minute break between classes when I'd see my friends. We'd devised a secret language that worked almost as well as talking.

A head scratch meant "What's up?"

A touch to the neck: "All's cool."

A hand on the hip: "Something or someone sucks."

When I saw Kade before last period, he'd added a new one:

Two fingers to the lips with a wink. My heart banged against my chest like a caged gorilla.

I watched as he walked away, his back straight, stride determined. Richie came out of a classroom and joined up with him. They walked side by side, arms brushing together, hips bumping as they jostled through the crowd. I wanted to be Richie just then, walking casually with Kade through the hallways of Kennedy.

One of Lawrence's friends, who I recognized from the post office parking lot, strode in their direction, eyeing Richie coldly. Richie swerved at the last minute to avoid a collision, but the guy also swerved—driving Richie into the chairs outside the counseling office.

Heads twisted around at the noise. I looked at Kade, who stood placidly beside the behemoth football player. Slowly, he drew his hand out of his pocket. His fist popped out, hitting the guy in the thigh. The football player yelped like a dog who'd had his paw stepped on. Kade retracted his hand, and I spotted the tiny stub of a pencil. He covered the tip with his thumb and kept on walking. The guy pirouetted on the ball of his foot to see who'd stabbed him, but Kade was already gone. And so was Richie.

I pushed through the crowd, trying to find them. When I crossed to the wing where Kade had his next class, I saw Richie wave and bound up the stairs. Kade was halfway down the hall, almost at his classroom, when Mr. Reid passed by me. He slowed about ten feet behind Kade and kept that distance.

Without warning, Kade turned around, planting his feet

shoulder-width apart. He stood in the middle of the bustling hallway and glowered at the principal. They squared off like gunslingers from the Old West. I hugged my viola to my chest as if I expected a blast to reverberate through the hallway.

But then Mr. Reid broke the stare. He turned and started walking back in my direction. Still frozen, I looked down the hall at Kade, who spun around and picked up his pace until he curved around the corner, out of sight. Mr. Reid looked me in the eye, nodding once as he moved past.

I was heading to my own class when the two officers from the assembly strutted toward me. My stomach dropped like an elevator in a bad movie. What if they'd found evidence, like a fingerprint on the handle of the storage-room door? No, we'd worn gloves. I didn't need to worry. Kade was always prepared.

I dove face-first into the water fountain, then wiped the water off my forehead and fell in step behind them as they headed up the stairs. A mass of kids coming down parted to the side.

The policemen were heading toward the art room. I was pretty sure that Richie had pottery and sculpture class this period.

It was over, I knew it. One by one, they'd collect all of us. The sound of the crowd dulled, replaced by the roar of a waterfall in my ears. I bent over, my head below my heart, and stayed there until the dizziness passed.

I couldn't believe my luck when they veered into the shop room. Kids swarmed the area like bees at a picnic. We didn't have to wait long. The door flung open and the crowd hopped out of the way as Mark Lawrence stumbled out.

"This is bullshit," Lawrence protested.

With the tip of his club, the buff cop—I think Mr. Reid had said his name was Officer Henderson—prodded Mark down the hallway. I was watching them go, trying to make sense of it all, when the other cop, Officer Price, stepped in front of me. "Let's go, miss. Show's over."

I lowered my eyes and hustled in the opposite direction.

Had Dave ratted on Mark after all? I couldn't believe he'd break the jock code of silence, especially after all this time.

The Kennedy High rumor mill lurched into action. Sidney Bishop told Nicole Haines that Mark Lawrence had beat up his girlfriend, who was recovering at Glenwood Community Hospital with a broken hand. I prayed it was true, because that would mean our plan for Dave had nothing to do with this latest development. But on my way to English, I saw Mark's girlfriend weeping into some guy's chest, wholly intact.

When the final bell rang, I ran home as fast as I could. I wanted to call Zoe and Nora from the privacy of my room. To my dismay, Dad was home. Just my luck—even workaholics took a break sometimes. I gave him the obligatory peck on the cheek and turned toward the stairs.

"Charlotte, I need to ask you something."

No, not now! I didn't want to think about someone else's legal problems. I had plenty of my own. Or I might soon enough.

"I have a new client from Kennedy High," he said. "Mark Lawrence. Name ring a bell?"

I shook my head, unable to speak.

"Good," he said. "I don't want you hanging out with boys

like him. He's been charged with battery against another student at Kennedy."

"Who?" I said, too quickly. I tried again with an indifferent tone. "I mean, what other student?"

Dad peered at me over the rim of his tortoiseshell reading glasses. I took a breath, loosening my shoulders. "David something or other," he answered.

I swallowed. "What happened?"

"I can't discuss the case with you, but I thought you should know that I'm representing the Lawrence boy."

"It's going to be all over school tomorrow," I said. "You can tell me the facts, right?"

He thought about it. "I suppose. It seems there was bad blood between them. David showed up at Mark's house the other night. There was a struggle, and Mark put him in the hospital."

"What did they fight about?" I asked, trying to repress the dread in my voice.

"That falls under the category of lawyer-client privacy, but I'm sure in time it will all come out."

I thought about Dave's parting words after he'd apologized to Richie. Something about having "business to do."

Dad climbed the stairs, stopping beside me. I edged up a step. A deep-set wrinkle stretched across the bridge of his nose, connecting his eyebrows. I knew that look: it was an intimidating tactic my father used to pry confessions from the scum of the earth. I recognized two other techniques too: "personal-space invasion" and "calculated quiet." My father labeled everything in an effort to educate me, but he forgot that I knew all his secrets.

I returned the silence, counting to myself in Spanish to make the time pass: *Veintisiete . . . veintiocho . . . veintinueve . . .*

Once people started talking, the game was over, Dad had told me. Sometimes they'd sink into a pool of lies until the only way to float to the surface was to reach for the truth. "Shut up or spill it," was what he called that one. Well, I could wait it out, force him to talk first.

My plan worked, and he buckled. "Are you sure you don't know these *gentlemen*, if I may use the term loosely?"

I countered his question with one of my own. "Is he hurt? The one in the hospital, I mean."

"Of course he's hurt, Charlotte. He wouldn't be in the hospital if he weren't. In addition to his already-broken arm, he has a busted knee and three broken ribs, but he'll live. As soon as he was conscious, he ID'd Lawrence. Other than that, he's not talking."

"That's too bad," I said.

"No worries. Jack's on it."

Jack is my father's seventy-two-year-old assistant. He likes to pull the senility act, asking the same questions over and over until the suspect gets so annoyed that he talks just to shut Jack up. The method's unsophisticated, but surprisingly effective.

I wanted to ask more questions, but I knew better. "Good luck with the case." I turned my back on him and continued up the stairs.

Our joke against Dave Harper had spun out of control. I locked the bedroom door behind me and did a belly flop on the bed. Don't cry, I told myself. It didn't work.

Dad rapped on the door. "Charlotte?"

I sucked in a breath. He knocked louder. With a sigh, I dragged myself to the door and flipped the lock. Dad pushed it open.

"Are you involved with one of those boys?" he drilled.

"Dave's in my English class. I don't really know him. Not well, anyway. But I can be upset that he's in the hospital, can't I?"

Dad's scowl softened. "You've got a good heart, Charlotte. I suppose I forget about the human element since I see this stuff every day." He lifted a hand to my cheek, catching one of my tears on his index finger. This little bit of tenderness made me want to bawl harder.

"You know, when you were little, we used to play chess together," he said.

I nodded, not sure where he was going with the trip down memory lane.

"You got very good very fast, and it wasn't long before you were beating me. So we entered you in a tournament, do you remember?"

"Yes," I said. "I lost all my games."

"Because you didn't want to hurt your opponents' feelings."

Huh, funny I didn't remember that part. But it sounded like something I'd do.

"If the music thing doesn't pan out, you could be a lawyer," he said. "But you'll have to toughen up if you want to be successful."

He walked away, leaving me to wonder how a person could practice insensitivity. I waited until he was out of sight, then kicked the door shut.

♪ CHAPTER 21 ♩

THE GLOWING RED NUMBERS ON THE CLOCK SHIFTED FROM 11:59 to 12:00. I tried counting backward from a hundred. I even did the counting-sheep thing.

"Forget it," I said out loud.

I should probably shrug the whole thing off. Dave was a jerk; he'd brought this on himself by bullying Richie. But still. If it hadn't been for us, he wouldn't be in a hospital with arm casts and leg casts and whatever it was they did for broken ribs.

I swung my feet to the floor. A pair of bloodshot eyes stared back from my mirror. I remembered reading that some of the world's top models spread hemorrhoid cream around their sleep-deprived eyes to reduce swelling. Did Tiffany Miller dab on Preparation H after a late-night make-out session?

The image occupied my mind for a whopping twenty seconds before my thoughts snapped back to Lawrence. He'd found the perfect excuse to pulverize an enemy.

But that excuse had come from us. No, from me. It was my idea. If it weren't for me, Dave would be at home right now. He'd still be a creep, but an uninjured creep.

I had to talk to Kade. The League didn't need to be like this— we only needed each other to be friends, not some vengeful mission. I knew Kade would understand if I told him how much it was starting to bother me.

I pulled a sweatshirt over my pajama top, dabbed on some lip gloss, and popped a breath mint before tiptoeing down the stairs.

The Acura was in the repair shop, so I rummaged through makeup, coupons, and loose change in Mom's purse until I hit the jackpot—the key to the minivan. Outside, I glanced at the carport and considered my bike. For a millisecond. It was definitely safer to drive a car than to bike in the dark. Sorry, Mom and Dad—this was a rule that required breaking.

The car started up, launching into an Ella Fitzgerald and Louis Armstrong CD. I ejected it and inserted the closest thing to cool I could find: Prince. That was as hip as my mother got.

As I backed out of the driveway, the car rocked over a curb. It was another mile or two before I felt comfortable behind the wheel of our giant familymobile.

I pressed down on the accelerator, glancing at the rising speedometer. I didn't even notice the Highway Patrol car until its blue-and-red strobe lights flashed in the rearview mirror. I slammed on the brakes without thinking. Thankfully, the police car swerved around me, on its way to something more urgent.

I took the parking spot in front of Kade's apartment as a sign from God, glad that no one was awake to watch my pathetic attempts at parallel parking. In the end, the fat butt of the mini-van stuck out into the street, but it was good enough for one in the morning.

Before I could chicken out, I ran to the building and buzzed apartment number 7. The call was answered by a click of the front door.

Four flights up, Kade's door was open a crack.

"Hello?" I called out.

His voice floated through the dark room. "Hello, Charlie."

When my eyes adjusted, I saw him sitting on the floor by the bookcase, the light from a candle climbing up his face. He motioned for me to join him.

Leave now! my brain ordered.

Don't be so uptight! my body said.

I sank to the floor beside him. "Did you hear about Dave Harper?"

"It had nothing to do with us."

"What do you mean? We made up the lies that—"

"Actions have consequences. And consequences take on a life of their own." His fingers spread over mine, dwarfing my hand.

"But we started it . . ."

Kade shook his head. "It was Mark Lawrence's decision. His responsibility, not ours."

I tried to read his face in the dim light to see if he believed what he was saying. He looked unruffled, as always.

"So if a drunk driver smashes into someone, causing a chain

reaction accident, then he's only guilty for the damage to the car in front of him?" I fired out.

It was true: I was my father's daughter.

The lone dimple on Kade's cheek seemed to wink at me. "If it works for the insurance company, it works for me."

"So I guess you're not losing sleep over this."

"Not over *that*." He curved a finger down my exposed ankle. "Would you like some merlot?"

I was about to ask what merlot was, but Kade was already at the kitchen counter, uncorking a bottle of wine.

A piece of paper poked out from under the bookcase. A word at the top, "Recommendation," caught my eye. Beneath that, a familiar name: "Richard Reid, Principal, Kennedy High School." I glanced toward the kitchen. Kade was pouring the wine, his back to me. With the heel of my sneaker, I dragged the paper across the floor. The letter was addressed to a Judge Michael D. Lombardi and the Walter Jackson Juvenile Detention Facility.

Kade Garrett Harlin has received three misdemeanors in the . . .

Something—or someone—had ripped the paper in half, severing the rest of the sentence. The next line read: "Expulsion from Kennedy High, if needed, and possible detainment at . . ."

"Guess the cat's out of the bag." Kade loomed over me. He handed me the glass of wine. "Now you know why Dick Reid's not my best friend."

"I didn't mean to be nosy," I stammered. "I mean, it's none of my business . . ."

Kade clinked his glass against mine. "I don't want to keep secrets from you, Charlie."

I took a small sip and decided I officially hated the taste of alcohol.

"I had a few minor scrapes with the law a while ago. Some judge asked Reid for an evaluation, and our beloved principal recommended expulsion from high school at the next hint of trouble. Seems he thinks I'm an excellent candidate for juvenile detention." He smirked. "My probation officer, Mr. Sterling, was kind enough to leave this in his filing cabinet for me."

"What kind of scrapes?" I asked.

"Stupid kid stuff. Stealing a golf club on a dare, a sandwich from the grocery store . . . stuff like that."

My eyes wandered back to the form. "Alleged assault" and "stalking" and "sociopathic tendencies" leaped off the page. Before I could read more, Kade grabbed it, crumpling it in his fist.

"Mr. Reid thinks you should go to juvenile detention for *shoplifting*?" I asked, hoping he would fill in the blanks.

He shook his head like he couldn't believe it himself. "Dick has a zero-tolerance policy when it comes to me."

He threw the balled-up paper toward the kitchen trash can. It rolled behind the refrigerator. "He better watch his back if he's going to mess with me."

"Over shoplifting?" I asked again.

"Idle threats," he muttered.

"But I thought you said he was after Richie?"

He offered me a hand, then pulled me to my feet. "We aren't

going to waste this lovely evening talking about that asshole, I hope."

I followed him into the kitchen, merlot in hand. As he opened a cabinet and parted some cans of soup, I poured half the wine down the sink, then put the glass on the counter. He looked over his shoulder, and I smiled, picking it back up.

When I glanced down again, there was a maroon ring on the edge of the white Formica counter. I reached for the paper towels to clean it up. Kade kept his place immaculate, and I wasn't about to reveal my slobby side.

As I leaned over to ditch the towels in the trash, I saw it. The oversized monitor had a hole in the screen. Its plastic siding, cracked. The keyboard looked like someone had taken a sledgehammer to it. Four letters were completely missing. I gasped out loud and Kade turned around, a battered shoebox in his hands. He eyed the remnants of his MacBook and shrugged. "It was a nice computer while it lasted."

"What happened to it?" It would have been in better shape if a Mack truck had run over it.

Kade slapped his forehead. "I was supposed to meet a study group at the library, and I was carrying it without the case. Stupid, right? I tripped down the stairs, and it went flying."

Wow, it must have really flown. Right into a brick wall. "Can't you get it fixed?"

"Nah, it's trashed. But it's OK. My parents will replace it."

I looked again at the broken MacBook, but this time, it wasn't the cracks and dents and shattered keyboard that caught my attention. It was the torn piece of paper. The missing section of a report. The report that was now behind Kade's refrigerator.

Kade took me by the hand, pulling me away. "I want you to know how much I trust you, Charlie." He lowered the shoebox to the table and flipped the lid off. "I've never shown this to anyone."

My heart stuttered in my chest. Not even Nora? I wondered.

He slid the box in front of me. Inside was a baseball cap, some jewelry, a pen, and a variety of other items.

"Does any of this look familiar?" he asked.

NEW YORK YANKEES, WORLD CHAMPIONS, 2000 was embroidered across the front of the cap. I'd seen it before. On Dave's head.

"This is what I call my success box," he said.

I reached for the lighter. "It's Zoe's, isn't it?"

"I really wanted the burned grade book, but it stunk."

Suddenly, I had no trouble seeing Kade as a shoplifter.

"You mean, these are from . . . ?" I hesitated, trying to think of a way to say it.

"Other plans," he filled in. "It's like getting souvenirs from the fair."

I cringed at the analogy. He made it sound like it was fun and games.

"Do you like that?" he asked. For a second, I thought he was referring to my glass of merlot, but when I looked down, I realized I was fingering a gold wedding ring on a chain. The clasp was broken, and the loose ends were tied in a knot.

I dropped it back into the box. "Sure. It's pretty."

"Take it," Kade urged, lifting it back out.

"No, I can't."

"Yes, you can."

"Whose is it?"

He dangled the necklace over my palm. "Yours."

I didn't want something that had been stolen from someone else, even if I didn't know the owner. But Kade insisted. I slipped it into my pocket. "Thanks."

His hand rose to my cheek. I felt my blood rush to his touch. Could spontaneous human combustion really happen or was it an urban legend?

"You know what's amazing about you, Charlie? You don't even know your potential. Once you find out who you are, you'll be unstoppable." He inched closer. I couldn't wipe the Cheshire Cat grin off my face.

"And, uh, who exactly am I?" I laughed nervously. I couldn't stop staring at his lips. They were slightly parted and flushed. And so close.

Without answering, he led me to the center of the room. My legs went rubbery, as if I'd just finished running a marathon. He let go of my hand, falling back onto his perfectly made bed.

I took a small step backward.

"This is my chair, my sofa, my recliner, and the place I happen to sleep." He reached back, tucking his head into the curve of his palms, watching me with eyes as deep as a cave.

"Come here, Charlie."

Standing there, with Kade stretched out in front of me, was making me dizzy. The spinning room seemed to rush up to catch me, and I sat down on the bed, dropping my head into my hands.

"Too much to drink?" he asked with a teasing smile.

I wasn't drunk, not from the sip of wine I'd had. Kade Harlin was the drug to blame. And worse, he knew it.

"Trust your instincts. You're safe with me," he lulled. "Close your eyes."

His reached up and closed them for me.

"I think I should go," I said. "Tomorrow—I mean today—is a school day."

"It's the weekend. You can sleep in."

It was Tuesday, but to Kade, the convenient response worked just as well.

All of a sudden his fingers were in my hair. I felt like I was going to melt like the wax dripping down the side of the candle. His hand closed, my hair tied up in his fist. My heart was an explosion of percussion. I hoped he couldn't hear it, but I didn't see how that was possible. My eyes were still closed, but I could sense how close he was. Very close. Then his lips settled on my mouth, as soft as I'd imagined them. Shivers rolled through every part of my body as I kissed him back.

It was better than I had imagined. For the first time in my life, I couldn't think of any reason to stop. Kade was finally kissing me, yet my stomach was in knots—I pulled away from him.

"I'd better go . . . ," I said.

"But you don't want to go, do you?" he murmured in my ear.

"I guess not," I conceded.

His kisses grew in intensity like a hurricane climbing the category scale. "This is going a little too fast," I said, forcing my eyes open. Kade was smiling at me.

Right now he thinks I'm cute. But it won't last. I can't hide behind my inexperience forever.

I took a deep breath and returned the smile. "I only said a little . . ."

He laughed, drawing my head to his chest. I rode the soft ripples of his breath for a long time, until we both fell asleep.

The pale light of dawn crept through the metal blinders. In a complete panic, I did the Limbo under Kade's arm, yanked my jacket off the chair, and dashed out the door.

In forty-five minutes, Dad would head for work with a briefcase in one hand and a bag lunch in the other. When he discovered Mom's car missing, he'd dial 911.

I thrust the key into the ignition, and the minivan sputtered to life. Twelve minutes later, I was home. I closed the front door behind me, listening for sounds of life. Nothing. My parents were still asleep. I sagged against the door frame for a moment, then returned the keys to Mom's purse.

Soon, my radio clock would launch into *The Steve and Lou Show*. A half hour later, a brown paper bag with a pastrami sandwich, five carrot sticks, and mozzarella string cheese would be waiting for me on the pass-through.

Nothing had changed, but everything had.

I got a whiff of something familiar as I crept past the dining room: furniture polish, eucalyptus scent. It smelled earthy, like home. I inhaled deeply until my sense of calm was restored. Then I headed upstairs to get ready for school.

♩ CHAPTER 22 ♪

TWO WEEKS HAD GONE BY SINCE OUR FIRST KISS, AND we'd hung out almost every day since. It was both wonderful and terrible, the latter because Kade didn't want anyone to know that we were seeing each other.

Our new relationship needs privacy, he claimed. *If you tell, it will change things.*

How? I'd asked.

In a million different ways.

That's fine with me, I thought. It's not so bad having him all to myself.

On a Sunday morning, while I focused on the piece I needed to know for the following week's lesson with Mr. Watson, Kade showed up. The usual way, via my porch. I'd been immersed in the frenetic world of Paganini, my fingers working hard to keep up. I jumped at the rap on my door, the bow flying out of my hand. It bounced on the edge of the mattress and clattered to the floor. I bent down to pick it up.

Kade laughed as he slid my door open. "That's one scary song. I could hear it all the way back to your fence."

Scary? I'd never thought of it that way. It was definitely a fast piece, though I wasn't even close to playing it at tempo.

Kade took the bow from me and placed it on my desk. He reached for my viola, grasping it by the chin rest. I held my breath until the instrument made it safely beside the bow. "No more practicing," he said, grabbing my hand. "Boring Sundays are a thing of the past."

"Wait!" I resisted his pull long enough to scribble *Going out, back later* on a Post-it. I slapped it onto my computer screen before succumbing to his strength.

Out on the street, Kade showed me his new Yamaha motorcycle—a belated birthday gift from his parents. I'd never been on a motorcycle before. I kept my eyes soldered shut the entire way.

We arrived at the entrance to his favorite place, then hiked up a steep path to the peak of the hill behind his apartment building. Lowell's Cemetery, overgrown with scraggly weeds and dried grass, looked more like a field than a graveyard. It was almost hard to believe that thirty-eight people from nine families were buried beneath our feet, but that's what Kade said.

"We should have a meeting up here sometime," I told him. "It's so quiet."

He shook his head. "I don't want anyone to know about it. Just you."

I lowered my eyes, amazed at how happy his words made me.

Kade lifted my chin with his finger, delivering a kiss that made my heart pound in my chest like a rainstorm.

When I came up for air, he said, "I come here when I get stressed. It chills me out."

I laughed. "You get stressed?"

"Certain people stress me out. Up here, I can scream all I want, and no one can hear me."

He pulled me close, his lips floating across my neck, my cheek, my ear. Whatever question I was about to ask drifted away, out of reach.

Halfway through Mozart's "Eine kleine Nachtmusik," Mr. Watson held up a hand. "Start again from measure three. And remember, it's an allegro. Lively, Charlotte, not a funeral procession."

I flipped the chewing gum to my other cheek and began, but my mind strayed from the page. I imagined Kade and me, embraced in a slow dance, his breath in my ear, body pressed against mine. Every part connected . . .

Mr. Watson flipped the music shut.

I looked at him. "What?"

"That was a soulless rendition, Charlotte. No confidence. No commitment. Have you been practicing?"

"Yes." Not much, but more than nothing.

"Well, it doesn't sound like it."

He removed the viola from my hands and laid it in its case. I gritted my teeth as he snapped it shut.

"Technically, your playing is fine. Emotionally, it's a flatliner."

What a jerk. One bad lesson and he was freaking out. This

was probably a sneak preview of what a career in music would be like—a ton of pressure to be flawless. Well, life wasn't perfect, and like Kade said, living your life was more important than music.

I grabbed my instrument and stomped out of his house, accidentally swinging my case into the shoe rack by the front door. Three dirty sneakers tumbled onto the floor. I didn't bother picking them up.

I was almost home when the mail truck pulled up beside me. I headed inside, flipping through bills, magazines, and flyers. Mom was vacuuming the family room, which was a good thing because she never heard my strangled scream. Leaving the rest of the mail on the counter, I took a furtive glance around and crept up the stairs. It took me a minute of serious breathing to open the cream-colored envelope with the raised logo in the left-hand corner. A flourish of a B trapped in a red circle.

Dear Ms. Brody:
We are pleased to inform you . . .

The acceptance letter from Barrymore slipped from my fingers, sailing under the bed. My dream—or rather my goal, as Richie would say—had come true, so what was wrong with me?

On 60 Minutes, which my parents never missed, a famous opera singer told Lesley Stahl, "Great musicians have to make music; they don't have a choice." Maybe I hadn't had a choice either—but not for the reasons she'd meant. What if Kade had been right about my parents, that the dream had belonged to them all along? Was it possible, as much as I'd resisted admitting it, that my viola had simply been a filler for an empty existence? Since my social life had picked up, I'd barely clocked three hours of practice time. Maybe, in the end, Kade had known me better than I'd known myself—music wasn't what I really wanted.

I stuffed the letter under a book of Vivaldi concertos. Maybe I'd take another look at it in a week or so. Or maybe I wouldn't. Whatever, I didn't want it staring me in the face.

One day, when you're happy doing something else, you'll thank Kade for his candor, I thought to myself as I left the room.

A week later, Mr. Watson called. I got lucky; Dad was at work, and Mom at a dentist appointment.

"Charlotte, are you all right?" he asked the answering machine. "It's not like you to miss your lesson . . ."

I was suddenly bone tired. Tired of Mr. Watson and all his demands. Tired of Mom and Dad expecting me to practice all the time so I could become a musician and play with some lame orchestra in some lame town.

As soon as Mr. Watson finished his epic message, I hit the erase button.

When the phone rang during dinner, I leaped out of my chair. "Hello?" I mumbled, gnawing fast on a tough piece of steak.

"Charlotte? Thank goodness I've reached you. I was getting concerned," Mr. Watson said.

"Uh-huh," I responded.

Mom and Dad glanced up from their plates. I turned my back

to them, cupping a hand around the receiver. "I'm fine. Really. I just need a break. When I find the missing passion in my life, I'll let you know." I hung up.

"Who was that?" Dad asked when I sat back down again.

"Nobody." I stabbed a fork into my asparagus.

I couldn't pretend to be someone I wasn't. Not for my music teacher. Not for my parents. Not even for myself. My stomach heaved, threatening to revolt. I didn't remember to excuse myself until I was halfway up the stairs.

♪ CHAPTER 23 ♪

SNEAKING AROUND WITH KADE WAS FUN, BUT IT WAS GET-
ting harder to hide the crazy joy I felt inside. We'd been seeing
each other for almost six weeks now, but no one else knew. If
it were up to me, I'd blurt the news over the PA system. Then
Kade and I could hold hands and stroll through the hallway like
a normal couple.

When Zoe called to invite me over for a sleepover, I knew I
was in trouble. Even so, I agreed.

When we hung up, I ran to the banister. "Hey, Mom!"

She appeared at the stairs, different-size knitting needles in
her hand. "What's wrong?"

"Remember that girl I told you about, the one who's helping
me with those logarithms? She invited me for a sleepover on
Saturday with this other girl, Nora, OK?"

"Whoa. Slow down. Does she have a name?"

"Zoe."

"I didn't realize she was a friend," Mom said.

"She wasn't, but now she is."

"Well, I haven't met Zoe's parents . . ."

And if I could help it, she never would. "Mom, I'm a senior. I'll be on my own in a few months. Can't you trust my judgment?"

I felt guilty saying this. I'd never been less trustworthy. But it worked. Mom's face crumpled, the giveaway that she was thinking about college. Me, going away. I'd seen the book in her bedroom: *Surviving Empty Nest Syndrome*.

My voice got soft. "Anyway, her mom's nice. She's a manager at Safeway."

Or used to be. After the puking incident, Zoe's mom was put on "medical leave." Because of her many years of service, her supervisor promised she could keep her job—as long as she got help.

"What will you be doing?" Mom asked.

"I don't know. Hang out. Talk. Listen to music."

"Oh, that reminds me, wasn't Barrymore supposed to let you know by now? It's already the middle of April. Didn't they say they'd notify you by the end of March?"

I smacked at an imaginary mosquito on my arm to hide the surprise on my face. I guess I knew she wouldn't forget about Barrymore, but I'd purposefully avoided thinking about this moment. Which left me totally unprepared.

"I didn't want to say anything—I know the waiting part is awful—but I think I'd better give them a call in case it got lost in the mail." That was just like my mother to want to take over, to fix everything. That's how she controlled me, I realized, through all her "help."

My hand tightened around the banister. I straightened with resolve, coming to a conclusion. "I've already heard. I don't think I'll go."

The words sounded faraway, as if someone else were speaking. Surprisingly, I felt nothing. Not disappointment. Not even joy at having made a major decision. Just nothing.

My mother, on the other hand, was feeling too much. She shrunk back, the knitting needles slipping from her grasp and clanking against the leg of Dad's recliner. "Charlotte," she gasped. "How could . . . ? But why . . . ? This has been your dream since the sixth grade . . ."

"Dreams change."

"But you love the viola!"

I glanced down at my fingernails. I'd never had them long, not once in my life. "Not as much as I should, Mom."

Her eyes roamed about the room as if it could enlighten her. "Does this have anything to do with these new friends, Dora and Zoe?"

"Nora," I corrected. "And no, it doesn't. I just don't have a passion for music. I think it's better to find out now than in my senior year at Barrymore, right?"

That gave her pause. "Have you thought this through?" Strangely, she didn't look angry. She seemed personally injured, which was worse.

"It's OK, Mom. I don't have to commit just yet. They give you time to think it over."

I thought about my acceptance letter, filed under a book of concertos. I hadn't noticed when a response was due. Not at that moment, anyway. I still had time.

"Let's discuss this with Dad and Mr. Watson—"

A wave of frustration washed over me. "It's my life!" I said. "Not yours. Not Dad's. Not Mr. Watson's."

All those times when I'd practiced instead of playing outside with the neighborhood kids, instead of taking ballet classes like other girls my age—that had been my mother's influence. If it hadn't been for her, I would have quit in the fourth grade when all my bow could do was bump into other strings—as clumsy as a baby learning to walk.

"My parents couldn't afford to send me to my first-choice college," Mom said. "I went to State, like everyone else in my family. It was a decent education, but it wasn't my dream. I just wanted you to have what I didn't."

My insides were a yawning tunnel, a feeling I could only label as homesickness. How was that possible with my own mother right in front of me? It felt like I was on a different continent.

"I know, Mom," I said. "But this is my decision. For now, at least."

I had a sudden urge to erase the disappointment from her face. Make her proud somehow. I could only think of one thing that would work; she'd love to know I had a "boyfriend," though the word felt too carefree to apply to whatever it was I had with Kade.

In the end, I couldn't tell her. Too much information about my life might put her in a coma. Or worse, she'd panic and share the details of my love life with Dad. So I kissed her on the cheek instead.

"Will you at least keep up with your private lessons?" she asked, curling a wisp of hair behind my ear.

I nodded, unable to wrench that last nail out, the one that kept her hopes alive. Although I knew it was only a matter of time before Mom noticed that Mr. Watson's bills had stopped coming.

♪ CHAPTER 24 ♩

BETWEEN THE ARMY FATIGUES AND THE HOMEMADE OAT-
meal and avocado mask, Zoe looked ready to hit the trenches. I
snickered.

"Shut up, Charlotte!" she said, tossing a wet washcloth at me.
"You're next."

Nora called from inside the bathroom. "Hurry up! This stuff
is drying out."

I stepped into the cluttered bathroom and eyed the bowl of
gook on the counter. "Yum, what's for dessert?"

Nora reached into her pink beach bag and brought out a box
of hair dye. "Copper Penny. Perfect for your complexion."

"No way!" I said. When Zoe opened her mouth to laugh,
hardened flecks of goop plopped onto the tile floor.

Nora tossed me the box. "Relax, Charlotte. Change never
killed anyone."

"You guys are ganging up on me," I moped. But secretly

I loved it. I'd done my time alone; having friends was a great improvement. They could dye my hair green if they wanted to.

Zoe took the box from me and flipped it over to inspect the shade chart. "It won't look quite as bright as the babe on the front."

I looked in the mirror. My hair was the color of a cardboard box. A little brightening might do me good.

"I'll give you a haircut," Zoe said. "I cut my mom's hair all the time."

Nora poured a smelly liquid into a bottle of thick cream. She covered the opening with her thumb and shook it like a castanet.

I made a face. "You sure it won't make my hair fall out?"

"In thirty minutes, you'll have gorgeous red curls." She peeled the gloves off the instruction sheet and put them on, then applied the gel to my hair. After she combed it through, she gathered the gooey mess on top of my head, securing it with a clip.

I frowned at my reflection. "Ah, the Marge Simpson look."

Twenty minutes later, I watched the stream of dye swirl down the drain. When I stepped out of the shower, wavy red strands clung to my cheeks.

Zoe reached for the scissors. "I'm thinking Hollywood-style. Side-swept bangs, that sort of thing." She nodded toward the Cosmopolitan on the back of the toilet. I glanced at the model on the cover.

"Anything looks good on a perfect face attached to a six-foot, hundred-and-twenty-pound body," I said.

"Jeez, Charlotte, don't you look in the mirror?" Zoe asked.

"All the time, but usually I regret it."

Zoe groaned. "Clueless."

"Why, what's wrong?" I leaned around Nora to take a peek. No food in my teeth.

"Nothing," Zoe said. "You're not half-bad-looking, that's all."

"Likewise," I told her. The look on her face said she didn't believe me.

"Copper Penny brings out your eyes, Charlotte," Nora said, blinking. She was having a hard time getting used to her new contact lenses.

Now that I was getting a makeover myself, I took stock of how much Nora had changed recently. Not only were her glasses gone, she'd started wearing makeup. Smoky gray eyeliner, and mascara, too.

I stole a glance at myself in the mirror. Trying to see how you look to the rest of the world is like working too hard on a report; after a while, the parts are an inextricable mess. My eyes were too far apart; my nose was nondescript and veered up at the end; and let's just say that my lips had landed me the nickname "Mick Jagger" in the seventh grade. I'd watched *America's Top Model* long enough to know that my features, taken by themselves, were part of the mysterious recipe for beauty. But somehow, they'd been randomly applied to my face, just off-kilter enough to blow the whole deal.

"So what did your mother do when you said you weren't going to Barrymore?" Nora asked.

I shrugged. "She told me to keep up with my private lessons, just in case." I hadn't told them that I'd blown off the last three. I couldn't bring myself to tell anyone for some reason.

"That's it?" Nora said. "She didn't flip out, scream and yell, or throw things?"

I laughed. "No. I mean she was disappointed, but she gets that it's my choice."

"Wow. I thought your mother was really uptight. Kade said your parents try to control everything you do."

Maybe my parents were too involved, but they meant well. I'd been pleasantly surprised by how easily Mom had accepted my decision. She wasn't happy about it—that much was obvious—but she wasn't going to keep me on a leash for the rest of my life, either.

Zoe ordered me to sit on the toilet seat. She moved the scissors through my hair, snipping fast enough to make me nervous, then stepped back to assess her work.

Nora whistled. "Oh my God. That's fantastic!"

Kade's words echoed through my head. *You know what's amazing about you, Charlie? You don't even know your potential.*

They shifted to the side so I could see the New Charlotte. My hair hung down, not out, in soft curls. Frizzy ends littered the floor.

"I don't look like me," I said.

The first time I'd met Kade, he'd said I was beautiful. Or something like that. I needed my friends to tell me how I really was, I realized. Being alone made a person too nearsighted to see herself clearly.

"You look awesome," Zoe said.

I squinted into the mirror.

Nora stepped in front of me, blocking my view. "Pay us back. Popcorn. Next to the microwave."

When I returned with two large bowls, Zoe and Nora were sprawled on the bed, cotton balls wedged between their matching salmon-pink toes.

"Better than going to that insipid prom," Nora was saying.

Zoe drew her foot to her mouth and blew on her wet nails. "Speak for yourself. Boys drop to their knees, begging me to go with them."

"We could go to the prom by ourselves," I said, climbing onto the bed. They curled their toenails away from me.

"I like Kade's idea," Nora said. "Think of the money we'll save. No tickets. No overpriced dresses."

Zoe wrinkled her nose. "I don't do dresses."

"What idea?" I asked, hurt that once again Kade had shared something with Nora first.

"Oh, he's got something up his sleeve," Nora said teasingly. "A huge surprise."

Zoe rolled her eyes at Nora's mysterious act. "Kade thinks we should skip the prom. The real one, anyway."

"He wants us to have our own party at this really cool place," Nora blurted out before Zoe could ruin her grand reveal. "Lowell's Cemetery."

"How do you know about Lowell's?" I asked her.

"It's his favorite place to hang out. Kade was dying to show me."

"Without me?"

Her smile vanished, and I realized what I'd said. Nora looked at me as if she'd stepped in something disgusting. "I don't know. Maybe you were at your *lesson* that day."

"Think about all the money we'll save," Zoe said. "We can eat and drink in style. We can even afford our own graveyard caterers." She turned to Nora. "What did Kade call it again?"

"The Prom with the Dead," Nora answered.

"Yeah, that's good." Zoe's eyes hopped from Nora to me, then back again.

Nora tossed a kernel of popcorn into the air. It missed her mouth, ricocheted off the headboard, and bounced into her purse, which lay open on the floor. A piece of paper, folded in thirds, peeked out of her wallet.

"You got a D!" Zoe gasped at the visible mark.

"You sound like I robbed a bank or something," Nora said.

Zoe fanned her face as if she were feeling faint. "You mean Ms. Valedictorian blew a test?"

"I can't keep up with hours of homework and have a social life, too. Those two don't go together, OK?"

I stared at her. "Aren't you worried what your parents will say?"

"I'm over that. Besides, I heard from Stanford a while ago. Early admission. There's no point in killing myself any longer."

"Stanford!" I cried. "I can't believe you didn't say anything. That's major."

"I accepted, but I haven't decided yet."

"Decided?" I said. "What do you mean?"

"There are other things to do besides college."

"Are you crazy?" Zoe asked.

What could be more important than going to Stanford? Nora had said there were 34,000 applicants last year for 2,400 spaces, and she was thinking of turning them down?

"Some of us can barely afford Community," Zoe added, resentment brewing under the surface.

"Maybe I want to travel," Nora said. "Become a professional poker player. Get a black belt in taekwondo. Be a screenwriter. Whatever. Live life." She stretched out a leg, kicking the purse under the bed. "Kade says you should find your own path and stop trying to be perfect by other people's standards."

"Yeah, right. Like he's an expert on perfection," Zoe grumbled.

"He seems to know a lot about life," I said.

"You should know. You've been hanging on to his every word," Nora said.

I looked at her, confused. Why was she angry with me when I was agreeing with her?

Zoe patted both of us on the thigh. "OK, OK, break it up. Who wants to play Truth or Dare? Or better yet, Truth or Truth."

"Huh?" I said.

"We're seniors," Nora said. "Not twelve-year-olds."

Zoe smirked. "Admit it. Neither of you has done anything worth confessing."

I swallowed hard. That would have been true a few weeks ago, but now I'd done more.

If you tell, it will change things, Kade had said. *In a million different ways.*

I reached for the DVD. "Want to watch the movie?"

Nora took it from me and chucked it back onto the nightstand. "You go first, Charlotte. I'll spill if you'll spill."

"I'll make this easy for you both. The answer is nothing and nothing," Zoe said.

The details of my love life were roiling inside me, on the verge of boiling over. This conversation wasn't helping.

"I'll bet my vintage army boots that Charlotte hasn't even frenched a guy," Zoe added.

"Not only have I kissed someone before, but it was recently," I blurted out.

Zoe shrieked with glee, then yanked off her right boot and tossed it at me. I wrinkled my nose like it smelled bad before pitching it to Nora, who made no effort to catch it.

"How long ago is 'recently'?" she said coolly.

I dug my toe into the shag carpet. "Well, um, I'm kind of seeing someone now."

Zoe's smile faded. Behind Nora's back, she shook her head.

Had Kade told Zoe the news already? If so, I didn't see any reason why I couldn't share my personal life with my friends. "It's Kade," I announced.

Nora stared at me, stunned.

"Well, we didn't want to tell anyone," I explained. "I mean, it's new to us, too."

The words "we" and "us" sounded weird. It had been "I" and "me" forever.

"How did it happen?" she asked.

"When Dave Harper was in the hospital, I went to Kade's

apartment." I heard defensiveness seep into my voice. "I had to talk to someone about . . . everything that happened."

"And one thing led to another," Nora said.

I felt like a balloon with a slow leak. "Well, I spent the night there."

"You *slept* with him?"

"No!" I backtracked. "I mean, I literally slept there. We fell asleep. I got home right before my alarm clock went off."

The conversation was like a game I used to play called Perfection. Thirty seconds to fit the puzzle pieces into their slots before the whole thing popped in your face.

"Just because Kade and I are together doesn't mean things have to change," I added, offering a feeble smile.

Nora's arm shot out and the bowl tumbled across the floor, scattering popcorn everywhere. She darted out of the room.

"Excellent work, Brody," Zoe said.

"If she was my friend, she'd be happy for me," I insisted.

"If you weren't so busy falling all over Kade, you might've noticed Nora's got a thing for him, too."

"He's not her type," I said.

"He pays attention to her. Believe me, that's her type."

What, was I supposed to hand over Kade because Nora's parents could only acknowledge her perfect report cards?

I held back my tears as we searched the house for her. I couldn't believe we were fighting over a guy like a lame teenage cliché.

"Did Kade tell you about us?" I asked Zoe.

"No. Your bug-eyed, lovesick stare did."

Crap. I'd jumped the gun, and now I'd breached Kade's secrecy rule. He was right; telling the truth had messed things up. What if they all voted me out of the League? *You'll be in the same boat as before, with no friends* . . . came a reasonable voice in my head. But that old boat had a crack in the bottom and was taking on water. My friends were keeping me afloat.

The backyard screen door slammed shut, rattling on its hinges. I leaped over a dirty litter pan and swung the door open. Nora was slumped on the bottom step, her face buried in her hands.

I moved closer. "I'm sorry . . . I didn't mean . . ."

I looked back to Zoe for help. She stood by the door, plucking dried leaves off a potted plant.

Nora leveled me with an icy stare. "What happens to our group if you and Kade break up?"

I didn't have an answer. For once in my life I'd been trying to live in the moment—I hadn't thought about the future. I didn't even know what I was going to do after graduation, now that I'd decided against Barrymore.

Nora stood up. "Just one thing. You should keep your eyes open. You might not know Kade Harlin as well as you think." She disappeared into the house.

"What the hell does she mean by that?" I asked.

"She's jealous," Zoe said. "She'll get over it."

She followed Nora inside. I stayed on the splintered, peeling porch and shivered in the cool night air.

♪ CHAPTER 25 ♪

ON SUNDAY, KADE AND I DROVE UP TO LOWELL'S CEMETERY. I tried not to think about Nora or any other girl. Right then, it was just him and me.

Kade collected handfuls of blue-and-white lupines as we wandered through the maze of gravestones. I waited for him to give me the bouquet, but instead, he stopped in the middle of our walk and hurled them onto the sunken roof of a squat mausoleum.

"Why'd you tell them, Charlie?" His voice was low, like a warning growl of a mountain lion. "Why'd you tell Nora and Zoe about us?"

His fury sucked the excuses right out of my brain. "I . . . I don't know."

Damn Zoe and her big mouth. She'd probably speed-dialed Kade the second I'd left her house. For the tenth time, I cursed myself for saying anything to anyone.

I reached for Kade's hand, which hung like an anchor at his side. "I couldn't keep the good news to myself," I told him.

His pale eyes turned cold. Glacier cold. "I asked you not to tell them."

"It's not that big of a deal," I said. "We're all friends. They should be happy for us. It had to come out sometime, right?" Whatever logic I tried to summon froze under his glare.

"You're wrong." Kade's words were like a snap of a dog and I pulled back. "Did you consider what I wanted, Charlie? Or were you incapable of thinking of anyone but yourself? Did you consider, for one second, what this might do to the League?"

"It doesn't bother anyone but Nora," I said defiantly, "and for all the wrong reasons."

Kade leaned against a tombstone. His fingers dangled over the etched design of a winged skull. A century of wind, rain, and snow had erased the person's name from the moss-covered slab.

"What do you mean?" he finally asked.

Was it possible that he didn't know about Nora? And if not, was it smart for me to tell him?

"What do you mean?" he repeated, slower this time.

I stirred a pile of leaves with my foot, avoiding his eyes. "I think she has a crush on you."

"Bullshit." He swung his boot over the dirt. A rock shot out, chipping a tiny gravestone. "Nora and I have nothing in common. You don't have to be jealous."

"I'm not," I said. "She's the one acting weird about the whole thing."

I waited for him to say something. He didn't.

"I'm sorry," I said, though I wasn't really clear why I should be. "Nora seemed really upset," I added.

"Don't worry about her. I'll smooth things over."

He moved toward me. Too close. I stiffened, closing my eyes out of instinct. I almost fell over when his lips made contact with my eyelid. I snapped them open.

"I guess it's not the end of the world," he said, his mouth parting into a smile. "You're right. It had to come out sometime."

His anger had evaporated as quickly as it had come, leaving my mind in free fall.

He started walking, his long legs carrying him twice as fast as me. "This place makes me feel like nothing in the world can touch me," he said. Our conversation seemed to fade like the names in the graveyard.

I tried to change gears, too, but it wasn't so easy. "Not even me?"

He slowed down, giving me a chance to catch up. "Present company excluded." He kneeled down in front of a tombstone and yanked out a weed that obscured a quote: ONE WHO WALKS IN ANOTHER'S TRACKS LEAVES NO FOOTPRINTS—PROVERB.

I read the rest aloud, MARY HUNTER, BORN 1674. DIED 1706.

Under that were the words JONATHAN HUNTER, BORN 1663. There was no date of death.

"What's the story?" Kade asked.

"Either he's in *Guinness World Records* as the oldest living male or he's buried somewhere else."

"Be specific," he prompted.

"I don't know. Maybe something awful—like he drowned on a transatlantic voyage, and they never found his body."

He nodded, seemingly impressed. "Not bad for a first try."

"Can you do better?"

"Next to the imagination, reality is usually boring," Kade said. "The Hunters bought this plot after they married. But Mary Hunter gained a hundred pounds and had one too many kids, so Mr. Hunter dumped her for a younger, hotter Puritan."

I laughed. "What a cynic."

I almost tripped over a tombstone the size of a brick. "These are the ones that get me," I said. "The babies."

Kade stepped over it, on the move again. "Back then, it was a miracle if a kid saw his fourth birthday."

He stopped in front of another mausoleum. Bouquets of plastic flowers lay on the ground, their cheerful colors leeched by time. Kade climbed over the gate, hooked me around the waist, and swung me over. He dropped to his knees, dragging his hands down my sides. I lost my balance and tumbled on top of him. In one fluid motion, he flipped me onto my back.

"Love the hair color," he murmured, nestling his face in it.

Kade was strong. Too strong. I felt claustrophobic and tried to wiggle free, but he had me pinned.

"I hate to ruin this, um, romantic moment, but my mom thinks I'm at Zoe's house. She told me to be home soon," I managed to say with the limited amount of air left in my chest.

"You need to stop worrying about Mommy and start thinking for yourself, Charlie." He adjusted his weight so that he was fully on top of me.

The alignment of his body with mine sent a shot of excitement—and fear—through my blood. Warmth and chill battled inside me. I twisted my head to the side to get enough air to speak. "Kade, my parents can't know what's going on. They might try to keep me from seeing you."

That wasn't true. Mom would do cartwheels if she knew I had a boyfriend. Especially one like Kade. Good posture? *Check.* Good-looking? *Check.* Polite? *Check.*

"Screw your mother," Kade said. He pressed my face between his hands and squeezed a little too hard. I couldn't turn my head. Then he scooped down, his mouth traveling up my neck to my earlobe. I felt the sharp pinch of his teeth and shuddered from the pain. Somehow, I managed to free my hand. I rubbed my ear until the sting went away.

Kade lifted himself onto his elbows and gave me the kind of smile that destroys any seed of anger before it has the chance to grow. "I can hardly stand being around you, Charlie. You really know how to drive a guy crazy."

He rolled partially off me as if it were the most difficult thing he'd ever had to do. I inhaled, feeling the sweet rush of air in my lungs. His hand slid under my shirt, tracing a figure eight on my stomach.

A few weeks earlier, the sum of my romantic experience consisted of a soggy six-second kiss from Jake Saunders in the back of the bus during an eighth-grade orchestra trip. Now, Kade slithered down to my belly button, making slow circles with his tongue. I fought for air like a nonswimmer trying to stay above water.

"Kade, I really should—"

"Should, should, should," he said, flipping onto his back. "*Shoulds* should be wiped off the face of the planet."

The world swirled around me as I staggered to my feet. "Really, I have to go."

"I know. I get it, OK?" he snapped.

My reluctance seemed childish, even to me. I was seventeen. But I didn't think I was afraid to have sex, I just wasn't ready for *Kade.* The insight left me confused and more than a little irritated with myself.

"Kade, I'm sorry . . . I . . ."

"Just forget it, Charlotte." He jumped up and started to walk away from me.

I scrambled to my feet, following him down the path to his motorcycle. He handed me my helmet. I took my position behind him and rested my cheek against his scratchy denim jacket. Gravel shot out from the back tire as we sped off.

A block from my house, Kade dropped me off. With a parting nod, he gunned the engine and roared away. I stood there, watching him get smaller and smaller until there was nothing left.

"Charlotte Brody, you're in serious trouble," I said to myself.

I walked home, careful to avoid the cracks in the sidewalk like I used to do when I was six years old.

♪ CHAPTER 26 ♫

OUR NEXT LEAGUE MEETING TOOK PLACE AT A RUSTIC CAFÉ on the edge of town, a forty-five-minute walk from school.

Nora and I were the first to arrive, followed by Kade and Richie. We sat at a circular table crammed with every condiment known to man. After we ordered, Kade looked at me. "So what do we know about Tiffany Miller?"

I felt a tug in my stomach. "I thought you said Wanda was next?"

"Change of plans." Kade turned to Richie for an answer.

"Popular. Beautiful. Ambitious," Richie rattled off.

"Manipulative," Nora said. "Slutty. Bitchy."

"Don't we want to wait for Zoe?" I asked. "She said she'd meet us here."

Kade glanced out the window. "She can catch up. Back to Tiffany." He rested his chin on a thumb, tracing a finger back and forth above his lip. "Vice president of the cheerleading association, co-captain of the swim team, part-time clerk at the Beauty Emporium . . . Charlie?"

"Prom queen wannabe?"

"Right. Good one. How could we forget her deepest ambition?"

I couldn't keep my eyes off his finger. He caught my gaze and smiled. My cheeks flamed.

"Tiffany's the kind of person who steps on other people's heads to climb the social ladder," said Nora. "I've never understood how popular and cruel can go together."

Kade tipped his chair back against the wall. He extended his legs, which didn't fit under the table. "Any ideas?"

"Tabasco sauce in her mascara?" Nora suggested.

The bell above the door jingled. Our heads turned in unison. Zoe stood there, hair hanging in strips, an open umbrella at her side. I looked past her, to the wall of rain outside the window. It was going to be a long walk home.

"You're late." Kade drained his espresso, then pitched the empty paper cup into the nearby trash can. He eyed the tiny puddles dripping from the spokes of Zoe's umbrella.

"Yeah, well, my mom was too sick to drive home from the movies, and her car was out of gas, so I had to take the bus to pick her up." She snapped the umbrella shut. "And then I had to walk all the way"—she looked at the log cabin walls, the remaining tower of biscuits and gravy that Kade and Richie had shared, the collection of tin coffee cups fixed to the wall—"here."

"You're always around for your mother, aren't you?" Kade asked. It didn't sound like a compliment.

"We were just talking about Tiffany," Richie got in before Zoe had the chance to sling a comeback. "We're going to do something to embarrass her, like she did to Charlotte at All-State."

Kade turned back, Zoe seemingly forgotten. "Good, Rich, good."

I looked away, thinking about the story I'd told. Yes, Tiffany had been mean, but nowhere near as cruel as I'd led them to believe. I looked at Kade and wondered if the truth would even matter now.

"Girls like her need to be brought down a few notches," Richie said.

Kade scooted to the edge of his chair, interested. Bolstered by the attention, Richie went on. "Maybe we can shake her confidence. You know, like in public."

"That stuff happened a while ago," I said, forcing the words out. "I've been thinking, maybe we should skip my turn."

"How can you say that after she ruined your chances for All-State?" Nora asked. She reached across the table to swipe Kade's toast. "It should be someplace where we can watch, that's what I think."

Kade bolted up in his chair. "The prom parade! It heads down Jefferson and turns onto Main Street."

The annual Kennedy High parade was this Saturday, April 28th —one week before prom. I looked down at my cranberry muffin, which I'd unconsciously mangled. The crumbs rolled off my fingers and onto the floor. "Isn't that kind of soon? You know, to plan and everything?"

Kade dismissed my concern with a wave.

"How come you always know so much?" Nora asked him, ruffling his hair.

I bit the fleshy inside of my lip. Now that she knew about Kade and me—and I knew how she felt about him—every touch was suspect.

Kade scooted away. Nora was too clueless to realize that he didn't like anyone messing with his hair. "They pass under my apartment every year," he said, repairing a spike. "It's a lot of obnoxious honking and waving from daddies' sports cars. I lock myself in the bathroom and try not to barf."

For the next ten minutes, they outlined ideas with a disconcerting amount of detail. "If we use the roof on the apartment at the corner, Reid can't tie it back to me," Kade said. Then he added, "Or you guys."

The new plan was based on his favorite horror novel by Stephen King, named for its main character, Carrie—an unpopular girl who becomes a school joke when she's elected prom queen. While she stands onstage, wearing a tiara and smiling, some of her classmates douse her in pigs' blood. Thankfully, we didn't have to slaughter a harmless farm animal—not when you could buy red paint on clearance at Grodin's Hardware.

Kade called his plan "Carrie's Revenge," because this time, it was the popular girl who was going to get it.

"Tiffany deserves payback, Charlie," Kade said, reading the hesitation in my eyes. Under the table, his warm hand cupped my knee.

I nodded, but I couldn't help but wonder, does she really?

♪ CHAPTER 27 ♪

KENNEDY HIGH WAS THE LAST PLACE I WANTED TO BE ON the Friday before the prom parade. The weather had finally changed, and all that sunshine was drying up my motivation. My grades were less than optimal, but with only seven weeks left, it would take too much of an effort to fix them.

Tiffany Miller declared that spring was here to stay by making her annual switch from Uggs to sandals with straps that crossed up her aerobicized calves. As I watched her glide through the cafeteria, rousing the male population from hibernation, I didn't know whether to be impressed or disgusted.

Nearby, the prom committee pecked at their salads while twisting sheets of colored tissue paper together. They hauled two trash bags, fat with paper flowers, out to the parking lot.

Kade said our plan would be a great show for all the people who hated Tiffany as much as we did. The weird part was, as we hashed it out, I realized that I didn't hate her.

I cast my doubts aside and headed to speech. As I turned the corner, Mrs. Roach, the school secretary, was stationed in the middle of the hallway, interrogating Zoe. I slowed, pretending to search through a notebook for something vitally important to my academic success.

"This isn't open for debate," the office ogre growled. "Mr. Reid wants to see you a.s.a.p."

"Sorry, no can do. Big test today," Zoe said.

"Right now." Roach took off.

Zoe exhaled an audible sigh and strode after her.

They passed by Richie, who flattened himself against a classroom door and stared at Zoe with deer-caught-in-the-headlight eyes. She glanced at him and planted a hand on her hip. The sign for "something sucks."

Don't panic, I told myself. But I couldn't come up with a single reason why Zoe would be called into Mr. Reid's office other than her involvement with the League. At least I could trust Zoe's loyalty; I knew that now. She'd waited a long time for her chance with Wanda, too. I didn't think she'd jeopardize it by turning us in before she'd had her turn.

Richie scuttled off to class, but I ducked into the supply closet across from the office and opened the door a crack so I could watch for Zoe. She emerged fifteen minutes later, not at all surprised by my sudden appearance. She tilted her head toward the stairwell.

When we were alone, she plunked down on a step. "Whew, that was close. I added a little zinger to my latte an hour ago. I was afraid he could smell it on my breath."

I stared at her. But all I said was, "Is that why he called you in?"

"No. They found my dog tag on the gym office floor."

"Dog tag?"

"You know, the kind they wore in Vietnam? You can order personalized ones on the Internet."

I stopped breathing mid-exhale. "Your *name* was on it?"

She shook her head. "I went for the motivational saying instead. Walt Whitman: 'Whatever satisfies the soul is truth.' Pretty cool huh?"

"I don't get it. How did they connect the tag to you if your name wasn't on it?"

"Apparently, Tags Express keeps records, you know, in case the police ever come calling."

The stairs buckled. I reached for the railing.

"I've got everything under control, Charlotte."

"But Reid's got proof you were there." I sat down beside her, sinking my chin into my hands.

"I told him I lost it in gym class."

"Did he believe you?"

"Who cares? It's all he's got, and it ain't much."

"Where's the dog tag?" I asked. "Did he give it back?"

"He says I can have it when he solves the case."

Maybe Zoe wasn't concerned, but I felt sick. We sat there, steeped in silence. Finally, I stood up. "This is the third time I've been late for speech. I'm going to get detention."

"Tell Ricker you have killer cramps and wink at him," she advised, saluting me with a scrap of blue paper. "Think I'll take advantage of this late pass and grab some fries at McDonald's. Want anything?"

I shook my head. She descended the stairs and left.

I was going to get detention, anyway, and there were only ten minutes left of class, so I parked myself in front of the trophy case and waited. Kade would know what to do. When the bell rang, I pressed my back to the glass to keep from being trampled. He stalked by me without a glance. I reached for his elbow, but he jerked away, reversing directions. He was moving fast, against traffic. I ran behind him to the practice rooms.

He yanked the curtain across the glass door and swept a music stand to the side. It teetered like the pendulum of a grandfather clock. I reached out, steadying it.

"I have to tell you—" I began.

"Zoe, right? Richie texted me."

"Mr. Reid has her dog tag. They found it in the gym office. He said—"

"Listen, Charlie. Until you know otherwise, treat threats like bluffs."

"But can't they link us to the . . . ?" I fumbled for the word, not liking the options. Vandalism? Arson? Crime?

"They didn't see her actually drop it," he said, impatient with my fear. "She could've lost it anytime." He turned his back to me, a hand on the door. "In the future, if you want to talk to me, leave a note in my locker. I don't appreciate you waiting for me at the busiest intersection in Kennedy High."

With a muffled thud, the heavy door shut behind him.

♪ CHAPTER 28 ♩

THE CROWD CHEERED AS THE SHINY CONVERTIBLES, COV-
ered with paper flower garlands, inched down the street. Prom
princesses waving in slow motion; the breeze flipping flat-
ironed hair into their smiling mouths. I bet they grinned in the
bathroom mirror to train their jaw muscles for the job.

I stood at my assigned post, waiting for my cell phone to
launch into the "William Tell Overture." Two minutes later,
trumpets sounded. "Hello?"

"Just saw Tiffany," Richie reported. "The boyfriend's driving."

"On Main Street, one minute and counting," I heard Zoe say
in the background.

I was practically spitting distance from Kade, but I followed
instructions and typed the text.

It's time.

My finger wavered over the Send button. I looked up to find him watching me, an eyebrow raised. I nodded once, then sent it.

He passed his apartment and headed for the building at the end of the block. Thanks to a wad of duct tape inserted in the locking mechanism, the door opened without a hitch. When he disappeared inside, I counted to fifty, then followed him. The spiral staircase, winding up six flights, reeked of urine.

Out on the roof, Nora perched on the half-wall border of an urban garden, her Hawaiian flip-flops resting on two gallons of paint.

"Nice day for a parade, huh?" she said.

I wished it were raining.

Stop it, Charlotte, I told myself, *Tiffany deserves this. Think about the spitballs in your hair, the ink-stained clothes, the insults.*

It dawned on me that my failure at All-State auditions had been more my fault than hers. I could have just blown off her stupid comment. I could have walked into the audition room, confident in my preparation. I could have tuned out everything but the music, and it would have all turned out differently.

"There she is!" Nora squealed, pointing.

The Kennedy High Marching Band blasted out "A Natural Woman." A string of cars followed the tuba player. Tiffany's yellow convertible was fourth in line. She waved to the spectators on her left, then turned to acknowledge the crowd on the right.

Using a pair of kitchen scissors, Kade pried the tops off the paint cans. He and Nora hovered by the edge of the roof. They held a gallon of Royal Red, waiting for their cue.

I knew this one act could stamp the "happily ever after" out of Tiffany Miller's fairy-tale existence. At least the high school version. It was powerful and unsettling to know before anyone else that someone's life was about to change.

"OK, I don't think—" I started.

Kade and Nora only heard the "OK." I cringed as cans of paint tipped forward, bleeding red ribbons down the side of the building. Without waiting to see the outcome, we sprinted down the stairs to the ground floor and flew out the door. Kade squeezed our hands before blending into the chaos.

I hid behind a telephone pole so Tiffany couldn't see me. But she wasn't looking, anyway. Her manicured hand slid over the bodice of her dress, smearing red paint into pink satin. Her boyfriend swerved the car to the side and twisted around, gawking at her. The paint dribbled down the sides of her car, and Mrs. Horton, the digital arts teacher, dashed over and tried to remove it with a wad of Kleenex.

The prom princesses craned their necks around, each with a pastel cell phone pressed to an ear. Their plastic smiles were gone, replaced by genuine expressions of pleasure. I couldn't believe that I'd ever envied Tiffany her entourage. These girls weren't anyone's friends.

Nora leaned against a stop sign, smirking with satisfaction. Richie and Zoe watched the scene unfold from the convenience store. Kade was supposed to be in front of the Laundromat, but I couldn't see him anywhere.

The crowd was surrounding Tiffany's car when I heard a piercing scream. I abandoned my post and stepped toward the yellow Volkswagen. Tiffany was as still as a portrait, clutching the shiny pink dress to her chest. All I could do was stare at the spaghetti straps of her gown. Cut.

I found Kade at his apartment door, the curved handle of the scissors poking out of his back pocket. Something black was clutched in his fist.

"What happened?" I whispered to the man beside me, keeping my eyes on Kade.

"Some guy in a ski mask gave us all a show." I could hear the smile in his voice without even looking. "He ran off before anyone could stop him."

Snickers from the crowd swelled to laughter. I closed my eyes, the only way I could think to give Tiffany her privacy. How could Kade do that? Nora's words echoed in my ear: *You might not know Kade Harlin as well as you think.*

If I asked him why he'd done this, he'd say he'd done it for me. But that wasn't the truth. It was for him.

♪ CHAPTER 29 ♪

ON MONDAY, I HUNG AROUND THE LOCKERS, WAITING AS Nora exchanged the books in her backpack. I wanted to make things right between us, and I needed to talk to someone about what had happened to Tiffany.

A few stragglers chatted in front of the drama room, but they didn't seem to notice us. I moved in. "Can we talk?"

She shut her locker and spun the combination lock. "I told you I don't care about you and Kade, Charlotte."

I shook my head. "Not about that. I need to—"

"Shh," she reprimanded. "Not here."

"Then where?" I whispered.

Zoe marched up behind us, startling me. "Glenwood Library. After school. I have to tell you guys something. It's important."

Nora looked at me and shrugged. We took off for class, each of us heading in a different direction.

· · ·

A teenager with dreadlocks sat across from me, rapping her knuckles on the table as she listened to heavy metal music leaking from her iPod. Her chemistry book was upside down. I almost laughed, until I remembered my own plummeting grade-point average.

Nora and Zoe were late. I figured I might as well get something done, so I looked up Shakespeare's love sonnets on the computer. When I reached into my pocket for a scrap of paper, my fingers hit something. I pulled out the chain necklace with the wedding ring. I'd forgotten about the "gift" Kade had given me.

In the light of day, I could tell it was too big to be a woman's ring. Inside, the inscription read FRANCES FOREVER, 1985. My throat tightened. Someone, somewhere, was desperate to find this. I shoved it back into my pocket.

Out of the corner of my eye, I saw Nora. She waved me over to a table by the young-adult book section.

"You want to tell me what's so urgent that you'd violate the 'no talking during school' rule?" she asked in place of a greeting.

"I need to talk to someone," I said.

I told her everything as quickly as I could. How I wished we could all be friends without needing a deeper purpose. How my doubts had grown as our plans escalated to new heights of . . . of what? Cruelty? What other word described them? She winced when I said it, giving me hope that she felt the same way. I ended my speech with, "You know I like you guys. My life's been great since we met and all, but—"

"What's your point, Charlotte?"

I was already regretting my decision to confide in her. "I thought I'd be happier when my turn came . . . I mean, Tiffany's turn."

"She sure deserved it." Hadn't she said the same thing about Dave Harper?

"Right," I agreed. "But . . ."

"But?"

"But it doesn't feel good to mess up someone's life. Even if it's someone I don't like."

"I hate to disagree with you, Charlotte, but the League's the best thing that's happened to me."

"You're right," I backtracked. "Me, too, but—"

"This is the first time in my life that I can be myself. The first time I've been able to let go without worrying that people will hate me for it." She crooked a finger around her purse strap and drew it close. "Kade knows what he's doing. We won't get into trouble, if that's what you're thinking." She studied me for a moment, then said, "Play along, Charlotte. The year's almost over. Soon it will be time for the Prom with the Dead, and then we'll all move on to bigger and better things, and you can forget all about us."

"I didn't mean—"

"Hey, girls, fancy meeting you here!" Zoe threw herself into a chair and propped a boot up on the table.

"What's going on?" Nora asked.

Zoe made a face at Nora's abruptness and reached into her camouflage jacket. She pulled out a piece of paper and slid it across the table. Nora and I looked down at a printout of a news article from a three-year-old Sunday edition of the *Highlander Times*. The headline stared me in the eye: "Girl, 14, Assaulted After School."

"Read it," Zoe urged.

"Quiet!" hissed a lady behind us. Nora tossed a curdling look over her shoulder.

A girl had taken a shortcut through the woods on her way home from school when someone wearing a ski mask attacked her. She was in the hospital at the time the article went to print but would probably be released in a day or two. Neither her family nor the police could get her to talk.

"What's this mean?" I asked.

"The unnamed juvenile was Jenny Carson, otherwise known as Kade's love interest from his old school," Zoe explained.

"The one who plastered his poems everywhere?" I asked.

She flipped the top page over. A second article was stapled behind it. "There's more."

I tapped the papers with my finger, delaying. My eyes wandered across the room to a couple making out by a magazine rack and the librarian shooting them a stern look from behind the information desk. Eventually, my eyes pulled back to the page, unable to fight it.

Two days had gone by. The police had a suspect, an unidentified student from the victim's school.

"This is ridiculous," Nora sputtered. "Kade wouldn't assault anyone."

I had the uncomfortable feeling that I should have been the one to defend him first.

Zoe pulled her boot off the table and scooted her chair closer. "My cousin knows someone at Jackson High, who knew Kade at his old school. When I told her that I was hanging out with him, she asked around. She said Kade has a reputation for causing trouble. Apparently, Jenny Carson moved away right after the assault. My cousin's friend says she lives in New York City now." She looked me in the eye. "I'm sorry, Charlotte. Really I am. But I thought you should know."

I pulled myself together to look at the big picture. "Even if it is him, she dropped the charges. That proves he's innocent, right?" But my father hadn't raised me to be naive about the law. People dropped charges for all kinds of reasons, from embarrassment to fear.

"He probably is," Zoe agreed, but I could see in her eyes that she was saying it for my benefit.

Nora pushed back her chair and stood up. "Well, thanks, Sherlock Holmes."

"Maybe you could track Jenny down," Zoe suggested. "Just ask her what happened."

I gave a single nod but didn't answer. I wasn't sure I had the guts to do that, even if I wanted to, which I didn't know if I did.

"That's stupid," Nora said. "Either you trust Kade or you don't."

"Right," I said. If Kade had anything to do with this, he would have told us. He would have told *me*.

Zoe returned the paper to her pocket. "OK, just sharing."

I tried to smile. "Thanks."

"See you guys later," Nora said.

I closed my eyes and listened to Nora's high-heeled sandals tap their way down the marble stairs.

♩ CHAPTER 30 ♪

KADE WANTED TO TALK ABOUT TIFFANY AND HOW GREAT the plan went, but his landlord was painting the bathroom. He volunteered Zoe's house, because her mom was never around. When we arrived, though, her mom was passed out on the couch. Zoe stomped around, but her mother didn't stir.

"She was supposed to be at a job interview," she said.

Poor Zoe. I couldn't think of anything to say that would make it better. Kade just looked annoyed as the rest of the League followed Zoe to her room. But soon we were on to other matters, laughing and congratulating one another on Tiffany's humiliation last Saturday. I kept quiet, offering the occasional nod so I wouldn't draw attention to myself.

Zoe's news in the library swirled through my head, drowning out everyone's words. For the past four days, I'd done nothing but think about it. I stole peeks at Kade, but when he looked at me, I glanced away.

At a quarter to seven, Zoe suggested we get something to eat.

"How about Barney's Hamburgers?" Nora asked.

"Too close to school. Someone might see us," Kade said.

"I know a pizza place," Zoe said. "It's pretty far away, but we could borrow my mom's car."

I thought about Mrs. Carpenter, splayed out on the couch. She wasn't giving permission for anything.

"The good news is we can go and get back without her ever knowing," Nora said.

We were at the door when the phone rang. Zoe stopped. "It might be the interviewer. I've got to tell them she's sick or something." She waved us on. "The car's open. I'll be right out."

As I squeezed into the red Toyota, I wrinkled my nose. The car smelled like it had been doused in perfume.

Richie looked back at me from the front passenger seat. "Where's your purse?"

"Oh, no, I think I left it by the TV." I climbed out.

Zoe wasn't in the living room. I glanced at her mom, spread out on her back, hands resting on her stomach like Snow White awaiting her true love's kiss. The real picture couldn't be further from the truth.

A voice was speaking on the answering machine. "Mrs. Carpenter, as we explained yesterday, serious action will be taken if we don't receive your credit card payment within—"

As I reached for my purse, I heard the unmistakable sound of Zoe's boots clomping down the hall. I hitched my purse onto a shoulder and ran out the door. I glanced at the car to make sure no one was looking, then peeked around the window frame.

Zoe shook out a worn white blanket and tucked it around her mother. She leaned down, kissing her on the forehead.

I managed to dive into the car without getting caught. A minute later, Zoe climbed in behind the wheel.

"Is your mom going to be OK?" Richie asked.

She started the ignition. "She's my mother, not the other way around."

"You deserve to live your life," Kade said.

In the backseat, Nora, pressed like a postage stamp to Kade's side, whispered in his ear. I leaned to the left, straining to hear.

"Can you believe my math teacher taught the entire day with two different shoes on her feet?" She described each sneaker in nauseating detail, punctuating the story with pats on Kade's wrist. He didn't seem to be listening; he just gazed past her, out the window, stroking his upper lip. Nora, lost in her own dramatics, dived into chapter two of her fascinating tale.

I turned to my own window and counted the passing cars with out-of-state license plates. If Nora had any doubts about Kade, it wasn't apparent. Out of the corner of my eye, I saw her flip her hair back and giggle at something he'd said.

Without warning, Kade's arm curved around my shoulders, drawing me close. Nora pretended to study something fascinating out the front window, but I could tell she was keeping tabs on us. Two can play this game, I thought, resting my head on Kade's shoulder. When I peeked at Nora, Kade's mouth twitched at the corners, giving in to a full grin. He was on to us, and enjoying the performance. For some reason, that knowledge made me feel worse. I pulled back and pressed my forehead against the window.

Trees and cars blurred together. Zoe was speeding on the two-lane road. "Aren't you going kind of fast?" I asked her.

A bottle of tequila, three-quarters gone, landed in my lap. "I borrowed a little something from home," Zoe said. "I don't think my mom'll notice it's missing. Not tonight, anyway."

Kade studied the label, then took a swig. "Ah, one hundred percent hydrochloric acid."

Zoe flopped an arm back. He dropped the bottle into her hand, and she took a swig. "Everyone's a critic," she said, then burped.

"Charlotte, you want some, don't you?" Nora asked, sweet as rat poison.

I didn't answer.

"Drink up, Charlotte," Zoe said, handing it back again. "You seem a little tense."

"No thanks."

Kade downed a second shot and passed it to Nora.

When the bottle had gone full circle, Zoe offered it again, this time with a hint of apology. "Last chance, Charlotte."

"I don't like the taste of alcohol."

Zoe laughed. "Who said it was about taste?" The car crossed the solid line, then settled back on the right side.

I'd just finished my driver's training course nine months earlier. All the endless laws I'd had to memorize looped through my head: driving under the influence; open container in the car;

driving more than fifteen miles per hour above the speed limit. I refused to dwell on the mangled pickup truck the police department had towed to the field outside my old school, a visual warning about drunk driving.

Zoe eyed me in the mirror. "Relax, Charlotte, I'm not even tipsy."

"Can you drop me off at home?" I whispered.

"I'm OK. Really."

"It's not that," I lied. "My parents made me sign a contract that I would never get in the car with . . . someone who's been drinking."

Had I really just said that? I slumped down in the seat, reaching instinctively to check that my seat belt was in place.

"Zoe's fine," Kade said. "Don't you think it's time you thought for yourself?"

I *was* thinking for myself. I wanted out. But I didn't have a clue how to do it.

"We're almost there, Charlie," Kade said.

The flimsy arrow on the speedometer hovered near 100, probably the maximum speed of the tinny car.

"I don't think I ever told you guys the real reason Wanda hates my guts." Zoe squeezed the wheel as if that would take the swerve out of the car. "I didn't feel like spilling my private life, way back when, before I knew you all."

Kade stiffened. "You trust us now, though, right, Zoe?"

She didn't seem to hear him. "It's my mom's fault. Like everything else. She went barhopping with the girls one evening and picked herself up a nice stud for the evening. Too drunk to even notice that she'd seen him before. Who knows where, right? Maybe at the science fair. Or school assembly. Or a birthday party somewhere. She was too drunk to remember he was a parent at my school. As for him, well, he just didn't give a damn."

"Wanda's father?" Nora gasped.

"Turns out her mother's a well-bred, respectable Christian woman. Sinners don't get second chances in that family."

The light ahead of us switched to red. Zoe slammed on the brakes, screeching to a stop in the middle of the intersection. She moved the gear into reverse and inched back. Luckily, no one was on the road to witness it. Or get in our way.

"Of course, when Wanda found out who the home wrecker was, she told me my alkie mother had ruined her family. So that's why she despises me and always will."

Despite my fear of becoming an accident statistic, her words flipped a switch inside me, leaving only pity.

"Your mother's the one who screwed up, not you," Richie said.

"Wanda blames you for what her father did," Kade said. "But we'll set her straight."

The light changed to green, and Zoe started up again, her foot heavy on the gas pedal. "The restaurant's about a mile from here. ETA: three seconds." She chuckled to herself, then jerked the wheel to the right, overcorrecting. The tires crunched onto the gravel shoulder before she steered back onto the road.

I imagined my mother answering the phone. "Your daughter's been in a serious accident, Mrs. Brody. I'm afraid the news isn't good."

This whole car ride was a metaphor for my life. Someone else at the wheel. Me, stuck nearby, helpless. First, there was my parents, always telling me what to do and how to do it. And then there was Kade.

Kade. Always telling me what to do. And me, always doing it.

Zoe glanced into the rearview mirror. Our eyes connected. The arrow on the speedometer dropped to a positively sluggish seventy miles per hour.

"Charlotte, it's OK," Richie assured me. "We're going the speed limit."

Times two, I thought. But the entrance sign to Paul's Pizza Kitchen, only a block away, made me feel a lot better.

Zoe turned into the parking lot and cut the motor. She met my eyes, hesitating a moment before depositing the car keys in my lap.

Thanks, I mouthed. I pocketed them and crawled over Kade and Nora to get out of the Corolla.

As the hostess led us to our table, Kade's eyes leaped about the room. He sent Zoe a scathing look and ducked down in his chair like a criminal hiding from the authorities.

"So there are a few kids from school," Zoe mumbled, gripping Nora's elbow for balance. "Sue me."

While the others analyzed the menu, I went to the bathroom to splash cold water on my face. With the faucet on full blast, I reached into my jacket, removed the bottle of tequila I'd taken from the car, and poured the remaining amber liquid down the sink. A toilet in the last stall flushed. I dumped the bottle into the trash, rearranging the paper towels on top of it.

"Are you all right?" Tiffany Miller, of all people, walked up behind me.

"Yeah, fine," I managed. "A bug flew in my eye."

Her plump lips, lined in red, curled up. "Uh, right. So it's a guy, huh?"

"Well, yes—I mean no. Yes and no." I braced myself for the knife-in-the-gut insult to follow.

"Guys suck. I just broke up with one last night." She narrowed her eyes in the mirror, inspecting her eyeliner. "He wanted one thing, you know? When it came to anything real, like emotional stuff, he couldn't care less."

Tiffany dug through an oversized purse and retrieved a seashell-pink cosmetics bag. I watched as she applied cherry-red lip gloss. Then she handed me her concealer. I fingered it like it was a stick of dynamite. Besides, covering my splotchy skin with the tiny wand would be like frosting a cake with a toothpick.

"I'm sorry about the parade," I blurted out, well aware I was in dangerous territory.

I couldn't admit to my role. That would be suicide. But I had to get an apology out there somehow. Yes, Tiffany had publicly humiliated me—many times—but it didn't make me feel better to have returned the favor. And the worst part was that it had started with the All-State audition story. A lie, invented to impress Kade.

"I'm sorry it happened, too." She ran a finger over her eyebrows, smoothing them. "But you know what they say: 'What doesn't kill you makes you stronger.'"

"Right."

Tiffany packed the assortment of beauty products back into her bag. "You know, you're not so bad anymore, Charlotte."

"I never was," I said.

She looked at me for a moment, then smiled. "As for the guy who made you cry, life's too short to deal with someone who doesn't treat you well."

Kade treats me well, I wanted to say, *as long as I do what he wants.*

For the hundredth time, I thought about what Zoe had told me at the library, even though I'd been working hard to avoid it. Jenny Carson hadn't done what Kade had wanted.

Tiffany left. I turned back to the mirror, flashed my best prom princess smile, and returned to the table for dinner.

♪ CHAPTER 31 ♬

"HELLO?" THE VOICE WAS YOUNG, MAYBE EIGHT OR NINE years old.

"Hi. May I speak to Jenny?" I asked.

"There's no one named Jenny here. This is Becca. You want to speak to my mommy?"

"No, that's OK." I hung up and dialed the ninth number on my list. It rang once, twice, three times.

A boy, no older than the kid I'd just spoken to, answered. "Martin Carson speaking."

"Is Jenny there?"

"You have the wrong number." He sounded as if he was reading from a cue card.

Of course, it couldn't be that easy. This wasn't the movies. It took more than a search of the Internet White Pages to find a person.

Maybe it *couldn't* be that easy, but I wished it were. With each phone number I dialed came a twinge of disloyalty. What if Kade was right about my inability to trust? No, wait. Had he said that, or had I dreamed it?

I sighed. "Thanks, anyway." I was about to hang up when I heard, "Oh, I know, you're . . ."

"What did you say?" I asked, bringing the phone back to my ear.

"Are you looking for Jennifer Carson? She's my cousin, but she doesn't live here."

My voice cracked when I asked him for the number.

"She doesn't like it when you call her Jenny."

"Um, got it," I stammered. "So do you have her phone number?"

"I can't give it to you. Against house rules."

"Martin," I said, pausing for emphasis. "It's important."

Silence. "Her stepdaddy's Jeff Kringler. Look it up yourself." A toddler shrieked, followed by a click. Martin had hung up.

A minute later, Jeffrey Kringler's number was on the back of my hand.

"Hello?" This time a girl answered. About my age. I wished I'd rehearsed an introduction.

"Hello?" she repeated. "Is anyone there?"

My palms were so sweaty that the phone almost slid from my death grip. "Uh, yes. Is this Jen . . . Jennifer Carson?"

"That's me. Who's this?"

"My name's Charlotte Brody. I need to talk to you about—"

"We don't need anything," she said.

"This isn't a sales call. It's about Kade Harlin. You went to school—"

"Who the hell is this?" After a long pause, she added, "How'd you get this number?"

"I'm Kade's . . . friend." I held my breath and waited. When she didn't say anything, I added, "I heard what happened to you. The thing is, I need to know the truth."

"It was a long time ago. I don't want to talk about it, especially not with Kade's latest girlfriend. If you're with him, then you're as twisted as he is."

Latest. I didn't like the sound of that. Questions I wanted to ask came at me from all directions. Dodging them was making me dizzy. But I didn't have enough time to pick one, because she hung up on me.

It took me an hour to resuscitate my courage. *She won't answer,* I told myself as the phone rang for the fifth time. *I'll never know what really happened. In the end, maybe that was for the best. Three years was a long time ago.*

I was just about to disconnect the call when she answered. "Kade's crazy. And he's a liar. You can't trust anything he says or does."

"What?" I asked. But I'd heard her.

"I did something that made him angry. It wasn't nice, but I wanted him to leave me alone. I thought he'd move on to someone else. But he didn't. He kept following me."

I pictured the crumpled form behind Kade's refrigerator. *Alleged assault . . . stalking . . . recommendation . . .*

"Whenever I walked home, he'd step out from behind some tree," she said. "He'd just wink and walk away. If my friends were with me, he wouldn't show."

I listened for a catch in her voice, a stammer, a throat-clearing. Something to indicate that she was buying time to invent more lies. All I heard was fear.

"It was stupid to take the shortcut that day. I knew he was around. I just knew it."

My armpits prickled with sweat. "Why didn't you press charges?"

The article had mentioned that the perpetrator wore a mask. Jenny might have thought it was Kade, but unless she saw his face, she couldn't know for sure. Then I thought about the prom parade, and the ski mask bunched in Kade's fist.

"It's complicated," she said.

I was losing her. "Please," I begged. "Tell me."

It was so quiet that I thought she'd hung up again, but then I heard a ragged exhalation. "At first I was attracted to him. All that attention was cool, I guess. When I saw him in the woods that day, he said he'd forgiven me for something I'd done. He said he'd leave me alone if I kissed him. Just once, he said."

It sounded like something he would say. I closed my eyes.

"Go on," I urged. "Please."

"You won't understand."

I thought about how an ordinary look from Kade made my pulse quicken. "I think I will."

"I was scared, but I didn't want him to know it, so I did it. I kissed him." She gave a resigned sigh. "Then he knocked me to the ground. Hit me a few times and left me lying there. I had to work my way back to get help, which wasn't easy with a broken collarbone and a twisted ankle."

"Why didn't you tell the police it was him?" If it was him, I told myself.

"Because after it was over, he said if I told anyone, Hannah would be next." She hesitated a moment, then added, "That's my little sister. He said he wouldn't go so easy on her."

My stomach ached. "I thought he was wearing a mask."

"Yeah, a black ski mask. But once he knew we were alone, he took it off."

"If you didn't tell the police, then how'd they guess who it was?" I asked.

"It didn't take a brain surgeon to link him to the crime. All they had to do was ask my friends. But there was no case without my testimony. The charges were dropped, and our family moved to New York a month later."

My mind flashed to Tiffany Miller, covering her chest with the remains of her dress.

"I'm so sorry," I said.

"Don't tell him I told you," she pleaded.

"I won't. I won't tell him I called you."

"And Charlotte?"

"Yes?"

"Get away from Kade Harlin."

♪ CHAPTER 32 ♪

"YOU MUST BE PSYCHIC, CHARLOTTE," ZOE SAID. "I WAS just about to call you."

"Yeah?"

"Don't be mad at me."

"About what?"

"The dumb thing I did in the car yesterday. Thanks for driving us home. I guess I'm more of a lightweight than I thought."

I'd forgotten all about it in light of my conversation with Jenny Carson a few hours earlier. "I'm not mad. Not anymore, anyway."

"I'm lousy at the whole apology thing."

"It's OK, Zoe."

"Charlotte?"

"What?"

"It was a stupid thing for me to do. I was pissed—not with

you—and I just wanted to feel, I don't know, free, or something. I wanted to fly away from my life for a moment."

I'd thought about Kade and how he kept saying that next time it would be Wanda's turn. But it hadn't been. After Madame came Dave, then Tiffany. Zoe had waited a long time. "I didn't ask Kade to do Tiffany's plan first," I said. "I'm sure he's got something in mind for Wanda."

Kade always had something in mind. My stomach shifted at the prospect. I tried not to think about the next revenge looming over us. Over me.

"Oh, I told him it was OK to do Tiffany next," Zoe said.

"You did?"

"Yeah, I wasn't ready. Still not."

"Not ready? What do you—?"

"Just not ready. Listen, I don't want to talk about Wanda." She paused, then cleared her throat. "I want you to know that I'm off the stuff for good. I don't want to end up like my mom, great role model that she is. And I definitely don't want to wear one of those tags on my big toe."

"I'm glad," I said. I liked her, I realized. I really did. Somewhere along the way, Zoe Carpenter had become a real friend, not just an assigned one.

"So, anyway, you called me," she said. "What's up?"

I was about to tell her about the call to Jenny, but my story was interrupted by a ping against the sliding glass door, followed by a more demanding clank. I drew the curtain back.

"I have to call you back, Zoe." Even in the dark, I saw three white pebbles—the kind Mom used to mark her vegetable seeds—lined up on the porch. *Kade.*

As I slid the door open, I thought about Jenny. "Just kiss me once," he'd begged. And she had, right before she was thrown to the ground.

"It's . . . eight o'clock," I stammered to the dark night.

"On a Saturday," he responded. "You aren't going to make me beg, are you? Oh, OK. Please, Charlie, *please.*"

I peered over the railing. Kade fixed his wolflike eyes on me, then dropped to one knee, spreading his arms out in an exaggerated appeal.

Looking down at Kade like this, I couldn't imagine him hurting Jenny. There had to be more to the story. Kade made people feel special. He made *me* feel special. And yet, Jenny had seemed so honest. If it had all been made up, why would she have talked to me? I wasn't the police. There was no reason to resurrect a lie.

I glanced at my wrist, remembering when Kade had grabbed it to stop me from interfering with Richie and Dave's fight at school. But that hadn't been personal; he wasn't trying to hurt me. He was protecting the League.

Why couldn't I decide who to believe? Jenny seemed to be telling the truth, but whenever Kade was near, I couldn't see him as the monster she'd described.

I was afraid to be alone with him, but I had to know what had happened.

"C'mon, Charlie! I'm begging you. Haven't you missed me?" He flashed his biggest smile.

"OK . . . ," I said reluctantly, mad at myself for not being able to say no to him, "but only for a little while."

I scrawled a note to Mom. *Studying too much. Going for a walk to clear my head. Love, Me.*

I was halfway off the porch when Kade pulled me down onto the dewy grass. Tangling his fingers in my hair, he leaned over and kissed me. Startled at first, I quickly warmed to his touch and found myself kissing him back. A few minutes later, we crawled past the living room window and ran, hunched low, to the street. I hopped onto the back of his motorcycle, circling my arms around his waist. He revved the engine, and I pressed my cheek against his shoulder blades. I could feel the heat of his body rising through the leather.

We sputtered to a stop at the rusted gate to Lowell's Cemetery. Kade tipped his bike into a ditch to hide it from passing traffic. We hiked up the hill to an impressive marble gravestone, obscured by the drooping branches of a willow tree. The headstone doubled as a backrest. Kade didn't waste any time and dove into the hollow of my neck. Suddenly, I felt vulnerable, just him and me in the deserted cemetery.

"Can we talk?" I scooted to the side. "I feel like talking."

Kade groaned. He moved closer and nibbled on my ear. I tensed, remembering that time when he bit it.

I gently pushed him away. "Seriously."

"So, what do you want to talk about?" he asked gruffly.

His sudden shift in mood left me wordless. How was I going to bring this up?

Kade rolled onto his side, propping his head on a hand. "So what did Jenny tell you?"

"What?"

"Did you satisfy your curiosity?"

"I didn't—"

"Don't lie to me, Charlie." He touched the tip of my nose. "Don't. Ever. Lie."

"How did you know?" I asked, my voice shaking.

"Nora said you were determined to find answers, that you told her you were going to call Jenny and get to the bottom of it."

"That's not true!"

"She said it was all garbage, but you wouldn't listen."

"No. What happened was—"

"Would you like to know what I said to her, Charlie?"

"Nora and I never talked about what to do," I said. "I wasn't even going to call Jenny. I mean, I did end up doing it, but her story didn't seem believable, so I—"

"I said to her, 'Maybe that's what Charlie needs to do to find peace of mind. Maybe then she can finally trust me.'"

"I do trust you." The words fell flat.

"What lies did Jenny tell you?"

I took a deep breath. "She said you assaulted her."

"I'm not going to tell you who to believe, Charlotte. You'll have to figure it out for yourself." He sprang to his feet and started down the hill.

I ran after him. "Come on, Kade. I need to hear your side of it."

He scooped a handful of stones off the top of a grave and hurled them at a pigeon nesting on a battered fence. It squawked, whirring away.

"Jenny Carson had reasons to lie," he began. "She was with a college guy in the woods behind her house. Things got out of hand, and they started to fight. She ended up in the hospital for five days with a sprained ankle and a broken collarbone. But she told everyone I followed her into the woods and beat her up. She said I was obsessed with her or something. It was obvious she was making it up, and the charges were dropped."

He cradled my face in his hands. "She took advantage of my feelings for her and used me to protect her Neanderthal college boyfriend." His eyes grew misty and he lowered his head to hide the tears.

I turned away, giving him a moment to recover. How I wanted to believe him. But there were holes—no, canyons—in his story. I just wanted to go home, as fast as possible.

"I believe you." My mouth moved of its own accord.

"Thanks," he said, but he didn't look convinced.

"I told my mom I was going out for a walk. If I don't go soon, she'll drive around the neighborhood, handing out flyers."

Kade's eyes were flat, unreadable. I shivered, drawing my arms up into my sleeves.

"This isn't about Jenny," I told him. "I have to go. Seriously."

He didn't break his cold stare.

I lifted onto my toes and ran my lips across his stubbly jaw. Without comment, he turned around and started down the path again. At the bottom of the hill, he hopped onto his bike and started the engine, not even glancing back to see if I'd followed him. I leaped on board. We took off, gravel shooting from his tires like gunfire. When we reached my street, Kade parked three houses down and cut the engine.

"You want to get together tomorrow?" I asked, sliding off. He had to think that we were back to normal.

"Maybe," he said. His hand swung out, reaching for my shirt. I whirled around, pretending I hadn't noticed his attempt to reel me in.

"Bye," I called over my shoulder.

I listened for the grumble of a bike engine, but all I heard were crickets. As I walked down the street, I felt his stare pierce the back of my head. I drew my shoulders back, lifted my chin, and didn't turn around.

It wasn't until I was on the other side of my door that I crumpled to the floor like a bird that's flown into a closed window.

♪ CHAPTER 33 ♪

I LEANED MY BIKE AGAINST THE MAILBOX POST, MARCHED across the immense lawn, and pounded on the front door. An agitated "I'm coming!" came from inside. The door swung open. Nora, combing her fingers through disheveled hair, glared at me.

"Why did you tell Kade I wanted to snoop into his past?" I demanded.

"Dammit, Charlotte, it's Sunday morning," she complained. "Couldn't you have waited a few more hours?"

I folded my arms across my chest. She groaned, treading back through the massive foyer.

"I thought this Jenny Carson thing was between us," I said, following her down the hallway. "Why'd you bring Kade into it?"

Nora fell onto the couch, curling her legs under her. My new-and-improved assertive side was making her nervous.

"Look, Charlotte, Kade backed me into a corner. He sensed things had changed between you guys, and he wanted to know why. He forced me to tell him what Zoe said in the library. Come on, you know Kade. He doesn't miss anything."

She was right about that: Kade was a human emotion detector. He'd unearthed feelings in me that I hadn't known existed.

"Why did you tell him I wanted to call Jenny Carson?"

"I didn't," she said. "He must've made up that part to get you to talk. Of course, you fell for it. You always do."

I didn't know whom to believe. She swung her feet to the floor and stomped to the door. "Kade didn't do it, Charlotte. Maybe you have your doubts, but I don't. He told me why Jenny lied and how badly she treated him. He was crying when he told me, Charlotte, *crying*. That bitch made the whole thing up."

I thought about Kade's eyes welling up. How he'd looked down so I wouldn't see it. And he'd cried in front of Nora, too?

She leaned against the doorjamb, moving a hand to her hip. "Because I'm your friend, I'm going to tell you something. Your *boyfriend* made a move on me last night."

"What?" The word came out like a cough.

Her eyes filled with tears, and she wiped them away. As much as I didn't want to believe her, the performance—if that's what it was—was compelling. But I also knew that if I went to see Kade right now, he'd have me convinced that Nora was making it all up before I could get my coat off.

"Just tell me the truth," I said.

"We went to the harbor and climbed on board this empty boat. I think it was called the *Majestic Seas*."

"You're making this up. Kade wouldn't do that."

"He's only with you because he has to keep an eye on the weakest link. That's what he said. He told me that when you called Jenny, she said he'd assaulted her, and now you didn't trust him."

I shook my head, not because I didn't believe her but because I did, and the truth of it was too horrible to imagine. I'd only just told Kade what Jenny had said. Nora knew because Kade had told her some time between yesterday evening and this morning.

Like late at night, on the *Majestic Seas*.

Nora started to push her glasses up the bridge of her nose, but then realized she didn't have them anymore. "He kissed me, Charlotte."

Without warning, she shoved me out the door. I tripped over the chaise lounge, but recovered. "I'm the one he really wants," she added, swinging the door shut with her foot.

Moving through the hallways felt like wading through knee-deep mud. Everywhere I went, people talked about the prom on Friday: who was wearing what, where they were going for dinner, how they were getting there, and whose parents were out of town. It made me sick, mostly because I knew I wasn't going to be there. Instead, I was supposed to celebrate in a graveyard and pretend that I didn't have a care in the world.

Or would I? The last thing I was in the mood for was a party with the League. Maybe I could pretend to get sick a day or so before the Prom with the Dead. I could get so ill that the whole world would want to leave me alone, and I wouldn't have to deal with Kade.

At lunch on Thursday, I showed up at the nurse's office. She left me alone with the thermometer long enough for me to hold it near the heat vent. An hour later, Mom picked me up.

I slept through the rest of the day, then on and off through the night. The next morning at ten, Mom leaned over me to check the digital reading.

"Ninety-seven point eight," she said. "That's terrific."

"You have to stay home for twenty-four hours after a fever," I told her. "School policy."

Later in the day, Mom decided I was well enough to go to my private lesson, and since I didn't want her calling Mr. Watson and discovering that I'd quit, I agreed. In a few hours, I planned to have a relapse. The kind that required another day of rest.

Sorry about the prom party, I'd tell Kade, *but I've been really sick, and there's no way my mother's going to let me out of the house tonight.*

At a quarter to four, I announced I was leaving for my lesson. I abandoned my viola in a blooming rhododendron bush and walked out of the yard, down the street, past Mr. Watson's house, and into the woods behind the elementary school. I sat down on a tree stump and dropped my head on my arm.

At least the year was almost over. I could make it through one last plan if I had to. But I didn't really want to punish Wanda. What she'd done to Zoe was unthinkable, but revenge couldn't rewrite history, and hurting Wanda wouldn't make Zoe's pain go away—all it would do was put us deeper into debt with Kade.

Tears gushed to the surface, along with more unanswered

questions. Was Jenny Carson on a mission to destroy Kade, or was Kade on a mission to destroy the world? And what had really happened at the boat harbor between him and Nora?

Nothing happened, I told myself. Nothing.

The word filled the space in my head, blocking out unwanted thoughts. I repeated it until my body relaxed under a blanket of humid air.

A cymbal of thunder shook me from a semiconscious state. I looked up at the ink-stained clouds churning overhead.

All I could think about was my viola: defenseless and unprotected in the bush. I ran as fast as I could, chased by the rain, until I reached my yard. Dropping onto my knees, I crawled through the puddles, under the kitchen window where Mom was chopping vegetables, to rescue my instrument.

Up in my room, I grabbed a towel and dried off my viola case first, then myself. As I peeled the wet denim from my legs, the ring in my pocket tumbled out, rolling across the floor like a wayward tire. I fell to my knees, flattening the glint of gold beneath my hand before it reached the heat register. Then I threaded the chain through the ring and hid it under an overdue math graph.

I felt completely alone. Uncertain of anything. I picked up my instrument, tucked it into the crook of my neck, and began to play.

I hadn't memorized the concerto by Seitz, not consciously, but the bow seemed to draw the notes out. I remembered how Mr. Watson had played it for me a while ago, demonstrating how a wider vibrato would make the tone more beautiful. He was right. I didn't know why I'd never tried it before. As I played, I felt the joy of the piece for the first time. Like cliff-diving into a deep lake and thrusting to the surface again.

The tempo picked up speed as my emotions drowned out my thoughts, driving away the fears that seemed to tether me to the everyday world. The cold ugliness inside me melted, leaving a happiness that surged through my fingers. Somehow, my bow kept up as the music swelled inside me, filling the emptiness and making me solid.

That's when the realization hit: I *did* like playing. I hadn't known how much I'd missed it.

But do you love it? I asked myself. Not every minute, I realized. I detested the endless scales, the exercises, the measures that needed to be repeated until my fingers went numb, but I loved the music. The creation of something so beautiful, so perfect. And even more important, I loved how it made me feel to play it.

Kade hadn't known one thing about me—because I hadn't known it myself until now. Music was a part of who I was, and I couldn't be whole without it. He'd tried to take away what mattered to me most so he could step into its place and control my life without distraction.

The letter from Barrymore flashed through my head. I laid my instrument down on my pillow and rushed to my desk, yanking the drawer open and rifling through so many songs practiced, accomplished, and filed away. There it was, still in the envelope with a clean tear across the top. I slipped it out and read it, this time in full.

My heart came crashing down. I'd missed the deadline. How could that be? There had to be something I could do, something that would make it all better. I glanced at the clock. Barrymore was closed. It would have to wait. Later, I would try to beg my way into my rightful spot.

I returned to the concerto, my last source of comfort. My heart became the metronome, ticking an unrelenting beat, accompanied by the distant chime of a telephone: One, two, three, ring. One, two, three, ring.

A knock on the door. My finger stalled on a B-flat.

"Charlotte, are you in there? How did you get inside the house?" Mom opened the door, poking her head inside. "Your hair! It's wet."

"Mr. Watson wasn't feeling well. He let me out early." I couldn't hide the depression in my voice.

"Why didn't you call me? You've been sick. You shouldn't walk in the rain!"

"I'm feeling better, and it didn't start to pour until I was almost home."

Tiny lines darted from her mouth. "What's wrong with Mr. Watson?"

Why was it that every lie required six more? My brain, the remarkable fabricator, had short-circuited in the rain. I shrugged.

Mom shook her head, frustrated. "Anyway, Charlotte, some-one's calling."

I waited until she was gone, then lifted the receiver. Terrified, but with a tinge of hopefulness, perhaps out of habit, I said, "Hello?"

"Hey, Charlotte. It's Richie."

"Oh."

"Hi to you, too. Are you OK? I didn't see you in school."

"I've been sick."

"Listen, I was thinking about the Prom with the Dead tonight when I got this great idea . . ."

I glanced at the clock. In two hours I was supposed to show up at Lowell's Cemetery with my party face on.

"We could pretend it's like a real prom," Richie was saying. "You in a dress. Me in a suit. Kade will *love* that."

I winced at the word "love."

"Wearing a gown in a torrential downpour doesn't sound very appealing," I said.

"The weather's fine now. You can see the stars and everything. Come on, Charlotte."

"I still feel lousy"—I started to lie, but changed direction—"about a lot of things. I don't think I can come tonight."

Richie paused. "Charlotte, it's our chance to have fun. Maybe we can have a mindless night for once. Just enjoy ourselves."

I didn't say anything.

"Please, Charlotte. Be my date." Then he added, "Kade will be really upset if you don't show up."

I glanced away, thinking. How upset would Kade be?

"Please," Richie said. "Do it for me and Zoe."

"OK, fine," I said, defeated. From where I sat, I could see into my closet. The red bridesmaid dress I'd worn to my uncle Jay and aunt Lin's wedding was still there. I'd missed it somehow in my Salvation Army purge.

"I'll pick you up in my dad's behemoth Chevy at seven thirty," he said.

I hung up the phone. How was I going to pull this off? I hadn't even mentioned the prom to my parents.

I dragged myself to the banister. "Mom!"

"What?" she called back from the bottom of the stairs.

"Sorry," I said. "Didn't see you there. I'm going to the prom tonight, OK?"

"You're going to the *what?*"

"My friend's prom date has the flu. Richie asked me to go in her place."

"Who's Richie?"

"Just a boy. From math class."

"Oh, just a boy." She laughed. "I can't believe you didn't mention the prom before! It's a huge deal. Or at least it used to be when I was in high school."

My insides fluttered with anticipation. For a moment, it felt like we were talking about the *real* prom.

Mom studied me, her face softening. The wrinkle on her forehead went back into hiding. "Are you sure you're feeling well enough? Well, never mind. You shouldn't let a cough get in your way. I'm so happy you're going! Do you need help getting ready?"

The relentless fingers of guilt reached out, pinching my heart. I hated lying to her. "Oh, sure. That would be great."

She smiled. "How about that red dress you wore to Jay and Lin's wedding? You looked beautiful in it."

I'd looked like a stick of licorice. But tonight, it would have to do.

"Great minds think alike," I said.

♪ CHAPTER 34 ♩

MOM GATHERED MY HAIR INTO A FRENCH TWIST, ADDING A few ringlets with a curling iron. She stepped back to appraise me.

"It took me a while to get used to it, but I think that new hair color suits you," she said.

"Is my lipstick too dark?"

"It's perfect."

"Do I have too much blush on?"

"You look like Cinderella at the ball," she said. "Let's show Daddy."

I looked in the mirror, and for the first time, I saw it. Just a glimpse, but there it was all the same. I could see pretty with my own eyes. I didn't need anyone else's.

"What's wrong? Do you want more eyeliner?" Mom rummaged through her makeup case.

"No, everything's fine," I answered. The truth was, I wished I were going to the real prom, not some consolation party in a forgotten graveyard.

I heard a familiar clank against my sliding glass door. I launched into a coughing fit to cover the sound.

"Can you get me some tea?" I hacked. "My throat's dry."

"I knew that rain wasn't good for you," she said, heading out.

Once she was gone, I darted to the door. An appreciative whistle rose from the dark.

"My mom will be back in a minute," I whispered. "You have to go!"

Kade, halfway up the tree, looked unconcerned. "Make up an excuse, Charlie. It's party time."

I glanced behind me. "I thought we were supposed to meet at Lowell's . . . Richie's supposed to pick me up in ten minutes, and—"

He climbed to a higher branch, then swung his legs onto the deck like a gymnast. "I spoke with him. He's already there. Everyone's waiting for you." He inserted a finger into one of my ringlets. "You look very sexy, by the way."

What was I supposed to say to my parents, that my date stood me up, and I was going to the prom alone? Forget it.

He waltzed past me into the room.

"What are you doing?" I protested.

The door flew open. The steaming mug in Mom's hand tipped, dribbling tea onto the rug by the foot of my bed.

"Hello, Mrs. Brody," Kade said with a nod. "I apologize if

I scared you. I was trying to pull off that corny *Romeo and Juliet* balcony act. You know, with it being prom night and all."

"You must be Richie." Mom lowered her eyes. It seemed no one was immune to Kade's charm.

"That's me," he said, lifting my hand to kiss it.

Mom took in his sweatshirt, faded blue jeans, and Nikes. He shifted, blocking her view.

"I bet you're wondering why I'm dressed this way, Mrs. Brody," he said, turning back. "It's embarrassing. I spilled something on my tux and had to get it dry-cleaned. My mom picked it up after work, and I was hoping Charlotte could come with me to get it from her. We'll go to the prom from there."

"Would you mind if I get a picture of you kids before you go?"

Kade covered my hand with his. "As long as you make a copy for me."

I stiffened. His lies were landing in my mother's trusting ears. Never mind that I'd spent the past few months avoiding the truth myself.

Mom introduced "Richie," the world's most perfect date, to Dad. Then she arranged us in an awkward pose and snapped pictures. In between shots, she kept reminding me to smile.

"Gosh, Charlotte, we'd better get going." Kade eyed his watch.

His act was as contrived and sappy as the photos my mom had just taken. Had he really said "Gosh," for chrissakes?

"Somehow, I doubt my tux would fit you." Dad chuckled, rubbing his stomach.

I started for the door. Mom dropped a hand on my arm while Kade kept going. She whispered, "Richie seems like a nice boy."

Where had my overprotective mother gone? How could she not see through Kade's act? Moms were supposed to have a sixth sense about these things. How could she be so annoyingly on top of my every move and yet unable to sniff out his lies? And there was Dad, flipping through the *Wall Street Journal* while his only daughter left home with a guy whose last name he didn't even know.

She pressed a hand to my back and ushered me out the door. I jerked away, hurt that her maternal instinct had failed to kick in.

"Have a wonderful time, honey." She smiled at me, her eyes full of pride.

This was my last chance to stay home. I didn't have to go to the Prom with the Dead. It wasn't too late to turn back.

"I hope you have fun with your friends," she added.

Friends, I thought to myself. Is that what they were? I thought of Richie's phone call, of Zoe and Nora helping me dye my hair. It's just a party, I said to myself. If we all hung out together, I wouldn't have to be alone with Kade.

"It was so nice meeting you, Mrs. Brody," Kade said. "Time to go, Charlotte."

Mom kissed my cheek, and Kade and I headed for the sidewalk. When Mom shut the door, he quickened his pace, leaving me behind.

"What's going on?" I demanded, running to catch up with him.

"I've got a surprise for everyone."

"What do you mean?" I asked warily.

"We have a lot to celebrate." He turned around to face me, walking backward. "Come on. We only have a few minutes until the party starts."

Was Richie in on this? Why was he already at the party?

"Just trust me, Charlie."

I pictured him and Nora on the *Majestic Seas*, discussing my so-called trust issues. I bit my bottom lip to stop my imagination from taking off. Instead, I thought about my phone call to Jenny Carson. She was a complete stranger, and yet I trusted her more than Kade. And then there was Tiffany Miller, who'd turned out to be a decent person.

Who *was* Kade Harlin, anyway?

He was watching me, I realized, watching me stand there in an ugly prom dress, my high heels glued to the sidewalk.

"OK, I'll tell you the surprise," he said, stirring me out of my thoughts. "Remember how those guys tore Zoe's shirt off at that fake party Wanda made up? Well, Wanda's under the impression that her friends are having a pre-prom party at Lowell's. When she shows up, we're going to blindfold her and rip off her prom dress. She'll have to make her way back into town in her birthday suit." He laughed. "It's going to be hilarious. It's time for Zoe to get back at her for what she did."

I smiled weakly.

"Good one, huh?" Kade asked, searching my face.

I considered telling him I didn't like his plan at all, that I didn't want to go to the Prom with the Dead, and that I was done with his League. But now I had to go. I had to put a stop to it. I didn't think it would take much to convince Zoe that this was a bad idea. If she agreed, maybe Nora would, too.

Kade climbed onto his bike, patting the space behind him. I slid on and gripped his buttery leather jacket in my fists, intent on not touching him.

"Let's go," I said.

♪ CHAPTER 35 ♫

MY HIGH HEELS SANK INTO THE SLOPPY EARTH AS WE trudged up the path to Lowell's. I squeezed Kade's elbow to keep from stumbling backward. Near the top, he changed course, scrambling up a short but steep hill using exposed tree roots for leverage. I tried to follow, but the toe of my shoe caught on the bottom of my dress. He reached down and pulled me up.

Under the hazy light of the moon, I took stock of myself. The hem of my dress was in shreds, and my left heel was missing. The pearl ring Grandma Brody had given me on my thirteenth birthday was a clump of mud on my finger. At least I fit the theme for the Prom with the Dead.

Kade was on all fours, scrounging around a fallen tree. He pulled out a flashlight. The beam hit the top of a tombstone. It glistened in the mist. But when the ray of light lowered, I gasped.

Mr. Reid was slumped on the ground, tied to the gravestone

with rope. His legs twisted beneath him in an unnatural way. His head lolled to the side, and a thin stream of drool dripped from his chin onto his red-and-white Kennedy High logo tie. A purple bruise, shaped like the state of Texas, spread out from under a blindfold.

My hands started to shake as I stared at him. How could the principal be here? *Why* was he here? He should be at the prom, breathing down the necks of kids smoking in the bathroom. No matter what he'd done to Kade, the man didn't deserve this.

I shrieked in fear. "Is he dead?"

Kade kicked him in the shin. Mr. Reid moaned like a foghorn.

"Relax, Charlotte. He's got enough drugs in his system to keep him in la-la land for another four hours."

Mr. Reid gurgled, and then his chest went still. I held my breath until he sucked in air again. I wondered what Kade had given him.

A branch snapped behind me. I turned to find Zoe leaning against a tombstone, eyes on me. I stared at her purple satin bodice, the neckline a weave of white ribbon. Her chiffon skirt swept up at the hem. Lavender pumps, dotted with dirt. And Richie, beside her, decked out in a baby-blue tuxedo. He huddled on the ground, rocking slightly. About ten feet back, Nora, dressed in black, blended into the night.

"I didn't know he was going to be here," Zoe said, looking at me. "I didn't know."

Nora didn't say anything. I could tell from the look on her face that she hadn't known, either. Richie just stared at his feet and kept rocking.

Kade wriggled his fingers into a familiar pair of cotton gloves, the same ones he'd used to break into the school. Then he thrust his hand into Mr. Reid's suit pocket, pulled out the principal's iPhone, and tossed it over his shoulder without watching where it landed. "He won't be needing that tonight."

I watched as Zoe, her eyes on Kade's back, bent down to retrieve it. She slid it under the belt of her dress, unnoticed.

Kade turned around to face us, his expression eerily serene. "After my meeting with Reid yesterday, I didn't have a choice."

He sat down on a bed of moss. Like a game of Simon Says, we joined him, forming a half-moon circle around our school principal. My eyes shifted back to Mr. Reid's chest, rising and falling in spasms. I was afraid if I looked away, he'd die.

"He says that I'm behind a lot of things that have gone wrong at Kennedy High," Kade said. "All conjecture, of course, which isn't very fair."

It *is* fair, I thought to myself, because it's the truth. "He's going to know this was your idea, Kade," I said softly.

His laugh was hollow. "Now he's trying to expel me over something that happened before the League formed."

Richie tilted his head. "What was it?"

"Don't worry about it."

"But it's almost the end of the year!" Nora said. "Why doesn't he just let it go?"

Whatever Kade had done, I knew it was bad enough that Mr. Reid couldn't let him get away with it.

"You didn't tell me about any other plans," Richie murmured to himself.

"It was my problem," Kade said. "I didn't want to involve you."

Richie nodded, but looked perplexed.

"Did you make up the whole thing about Wanda?" I asked Kade.

"I had to get you up here somehow," he said. "You're part of the League, like it or not."

"I don't," I told him. "Not anymore."

"We've done too much together. If you tell anyone, we'll all get in trouble."

I swallowed hard. He was right, of course. He'd seen to it that the members of the League had participated in all the plans, that we were as guilty as him. "I won't tell, Kade. I could never ruin Nora, Richie, and Zoe's future." I looked at him pointedly and saw that the message wasn't lost.

Kade turned back to Richie. "Anyway, I'm sick of Reid hounding me. He'll never catch me, because I'm smarter than him. It's time to make that perfectly clear."

As I looked at Kade's calm, unruffled expression, I realized that what I'd once mistaken for confidence was nothing more than dressed-up arrogance.

"What do you want us to do?" Richie's voice was so quiet, I was surprised anyone heard it.

"We have to show him he can't mess with me," Kade sneered. "He thinks I'm guilty of everything bad that happens at the damn school!"

Because you are, I thought.

"If we take Reid home right now, he won't have to know

about this," I said, looking to Nora, Richie, and Zoe for support. Their faces were unreadable.

Kade clenched his fist at his side. I pictured the flattened Coke can. The demolished MacBook. The torn report beside it. Mr. Reid was suffering because he'd interfered, and next it was going to be my turn. I shut my eyes and tensed, bracing myself. Instead, I felt the whisper of fingers against my cheek, light as butterfly wings.

"I care for you a lot, Charlotte, you know that. We're all a team. I'm asking you to be there for me." He removed his hand, but the impression of his fingers stayed. My face felt dirty. I wanted to scrub away his touch.

"We're in this together," Kade said, addressing all of us now. "I'd never rat on any of you for what we did to Madame Detroit, or Dave Harper, or Tiffany Miller. We did those things for you. This time, it's my turn."

The cemetery was still. Even the crickets seemed tuned to Kade's words. Richie shivered, despite the mild spring night. When he rubbed his eyes, I stared at his hands, stained with dirt and blood.

"What happened to you?" I choked.

"I cut them on a board." Richie's voice was robotic. "I hit Reid with it so Kade could give him the drug."

"Reid was on his way to the prom," Kade said, smiling. "The Prom with the Dead, as it turns out."

My head was spinning. I wished I could just run away.

"What are we going to do with him?" I asked. "Just leave him here?"

"There are other options," Kade responded.

"What do you mean?" Nora asked.

"You're a smart girl," Kade said. "Figure it out."

Zoe, Richie, and Nora looked like they were at their best friend's funeral. Kade caught my eye and held it. The usual flutter in my heart was now a drumbeat of fear.

From behind his back, Kade brought out a rock and pitched it across the circle. It tumbled along the ground to Richie's feet.

"Oh my God," I said. "This is crazy. Haven't you done enough already?"

Kade ignored me. "Do it now, Richie, and he won't feel a thing."

I dug my nails into my palm. "No!"

Nora took a small step forward. "I know you're upset, Kade. For good reason. But maybe we can talk about this first."

How could she sound so calm? Zoe hooked her pinkie around mine and squeezed. I dropped my head on her shoulder.

Kade's eyes drifted to the rock. Addressing no one in particular, he said, "Reid told me he's been watching me and my friends. He's onto us. All of us."

I remembered when Kade said the League was for friendship and support. None of those factors had been a part of his formula, I now realized. "You planned to get Mr. Reid from the beginning, didn't you?"

"Shut up, Charlotte. You don't know what you're talking about."

"He's been following *you* around. He never was after Richie, was he?"

Richie's head jerked up at his name. I reached for a hand. Anyone's. It was Nora's. "Let's get out of here," I said.

She shook me off. "You can't just walk away, Charlotte. He needs us."

For a moment, I thought she was talking about the principal.

"Do it, Richie," Kade ordered. "Do it for me."

Richie picked up the rock, tracing the jagged edges with his thumb.

"I've always been there for you," Kade said. "I protected you."

"No, Richie!" I begged.

Nora patted Kade's arm. "Let's go for a walk and calm down. Reid's going to be out of it for hours. We don't have to do anything right now."

I understood Nora's thought process, but it wouldn't work. Kade wasn't going to change his mind because he had a few extra minutes to think about it. Who knew how long he'd been planning this.

Richie glanced at Kade, then at me. He flipped the rock in his hands, shifting his focus to Mr. Reid's dress shoes, which were crusted with mud.

"Friends for life," Kade told him.

There was that word again. *Friends.* On second thought, maybe the League *had* been about support and protection—as long as that meant taking the fall for Kade.

"Didn't you say that smart people don't get caught?" I asked. "Maybe that's because they're too smart to do the dirty work themselves."

"Shut up, Charlotte," he snapped.

Richie stared at his hands, refusing to look at me. I hoped I hadn't gone too far. The last thing I wanted was for him to jump to Kade's defense.

"Please, Richie, can't you see he's using you?" I asked.

Kade tuned us out, all except Richie. "They'll come to me first. Make me take a lie detector test. I have to be able to say I didn't do it so they'll leave me alone. So they'll leave all of us alone."

Richie mumbled to himself, shaking his head. The rock trembled in his hands. He scooted forward, kneeling before Mr. Reid as he raised it to his chin.

"Don't ruin your future, Richie," I told him.

"What future?" he asked solemnly.

I sighed with relief. At least he was listening to me. "Your restaurant . . . and the love that's coming to you."

"Do it!" Kade demanded.

If I had to, I knew I could rush Richie. Knock him off balance. But I also knew that Kade would have me nailed to the ground in seconds, just like he'd done to Jenny.

Richie sent me an apologetic glance.

"Who's your friend here, buddy?" Kade said. "Is it Reid, who turned his back when those jocks jumped you?"

"Or is it Kade, who's asking you to go to prison for him?" I finished.

Kade ignored me. "Think about how he treated you, Richie. Come on, wake up, man!"

"Who knows if Mr. Reid ever said those things about you,"

I said to Richie. "Kade told you he overheard it, but what if it wasn't true? What if he made it all up?"

Everyone was standing now, except Richie, who knelt in front of Mr. Reid, the rock shaking in his hands.

Kade stepped toward me, but Zoe moved into his path, fists raised.

"Tough as you think you are, I can kick your ass, Zoe. Don't forget that."

When Kade turned his gaze back to Richie, Zoe pinched my waist. I looked down as she tapped the iPhone in her belt. 9-1-1 glowed on the screen.

I counted to ten, then raised my voice. "You were the one who brought Mr. Reid to Lowell's Cemetery, so you take care of him! We don't want anything to do with this."

I didn't dare say much else. They always recorded 911 calls, and I didn't want my voice recognized.

Kade squeezed Richie's arm. "Come on!"

I looked at Richie. He looked away. "Think," I whispered.

Richie lifted the rock over his head. "No!" I screamed, lunging toward him.

Clunk.

Richie threw the rock. It ricocheted off the fallen tree and rolled into a bush.

Mr. Reid whistled in his sleep. I collapsed to the ground, weak with relief. Richie darted into Zoe's arms.

"You're going to listen to them over me?" Kade thundered.

Zoe hugged Richie, holding on tight like she was afraid he'd slip through her fingers. Nora frowned. She hadn't moved an inch.

"Let's get out of here," Richie said. Zoe released him, and he held out a hand, helping me to my feet. He looked at Mr. Reid, then back to me. "We'll call someone, get him help."

"Come with us," I pleaded to Nora. I couldn't leave her behind, not with Kade. Not with Mr. Reid still in danger.

"You guys don't know the first thing about friendship." She moved to Kade's side.

Richie shrank an inch. I tightened my hold on his arm.

Kade rested his chin on his thumb and ran an index finger across his lip. I knew the look: he was adapting his "plan" to fit the current situation, but first, he had to figure out what to do with his defectors.

A siren hummed in the distance, increasing to a wail as it drew closer. Zoe, Richie, and I glanced at one another, then ran for the hill, toppling down the muddy slope. Kade and Nora took off in the other direction.

Wild blackberry thorns tore at my arms as I broke through in search of another path. Somehow we reached the main road, with only enough time to dive to the ground as two police cars tore past. I lifted my head from a carpet of wet leaves when Kade's motorcycle roared by from the opposite direction. Nora was in my seat, her cheek plastered to the back of Kade's jacket.

When all was clear, we took each other's hands and walked home in silence. It felt as if someone had died.

Thank God no one had.

♪ CHAPTER 36 ♪

I SHOULDN'T HAVE BEEN SURPRISED TO FIND MY HOUSE all lit up at midnight. Mom and Dad were waiting up for me. There was no way I could let them see my mud-splattered, shredded dress. I snuck around to the side yard, hiking the gown to my waist so I could climb up the tree. Back in my room, I switched to a T-shirt and jeans. With my heart galloping, I rounded back outside to the main entrance.

"Oh," Mom said, taken aback by my casual appearance.

"I left my dress at Zoe's," I explained. "I'll get it tomorrow."

"Why aren't you wearing it?" Mom asked. "I was hoping for a few more pictures."

"I could only do the whole princess act for a few hours."

"So, how'd it go, Cinderella?" Dad asked.

"It was fun, but I'm wiped," I forced out. "Too much dancing to bad pop music. I think I'll head to bed."

Mom frowned. "But what—?"

"I'll fill you in tomorrow, OK? Right now, I've got a date with my pillow."

She gave a short laugh. I quickly excused myself and darted up the stairs before she could squeeze in some last-ditch questions.

In my room, I stared at my bed. I didn't want to lie down. If I tried to sleep, I knew all the horrible images of the night would haunt me. Instead, I collapsed into my beanbag chair and whispered a prayer for Mr. Reid. *Please let him be safe in a hospital. Please let him recover. And God, please keep Kade Harlin away from me.*

The next morning, while most of the student population was in REM sleep, I had my ear to the door, listening for the thud of Saturday's newspaper against the front steps. As soon as it came, I ran to my room and tore through the local section. No mention of anything unusual happening at the Kennedy High prom. I didn't know if that was good or bad. At least if the story had broken, I'd know whether Mr. Reid was OK.

My phone chirped. No surprise I wasn't the only one up at this hour. I ran over to it and read the text from Zoe:

just called the hospital. he's being released today.

I breathed a sigh of relief, then went into the directory and deleted the message.

When I came downstairs, Mom watched me too carefully. To her credit, she didn't barrage me with questions. She just disappeared into the kitchen, probably to retrieve one of her megavitamins with extra B-12 for energy.

A minute later, she was back. "Need a lift?" she asked, holding out a steaming mug of coffee. A full cup. The real deal. Coming from her, it was like the elixir of life.

Tears stung my eyes but refused to make an appearance. "You're the best, Mom," I said.

She brought a hand to her cheek. "I haven't heard you say that since you were five years old. If I'd known, I would've put coffee in your sippy cup."

I laid my head in her lap as she scratched my back. She hadn't done that since I was five, either.

"The last few weeks of school are tough on everyone," she said. "I'm not too old to remember."

Her words brought back my problems. If Mr. Reid figured out who his abductors were, none of us would graduate from high school.

I gulped down the coffee, gave Mom a hug, and lumbered upstairs to look for some industrial-strength makeup to hide the circles under my eyes.

I was scared to go to school, for a lot of reasons, but becoming a hermit for the rest of my life wasn't an option.

In chemistry, I sat on the edge of my seat, waiting for the intercom to announce an emergency assembly. It didn't come. No news is good news, I told myself. But that wasn't true; no news could mean they were busy gathering evidence.

While Mrs. Stanton droned on about the definition of kinetic theory, I thought about how Kade got Jenny Carson to kiss him in the woods that day. He'd trapped her with a mix of seduction and fear, the formula achingly familiar.

I drew a map to and from my classes that would put me the farthest distance from Kade. But on my way to orchestra, he materialized from an empty classroom.

"We have to talk. Can you stop by my apartment after school?"

"I don't think so."

"Come on, Charlie, we can work this out. I explained it all to Nora. It's just a big misunderstanding. See, I was angry at Reid for all the awful things he'd done to me, but I only wanted Richie to hurt him, not kill him or anything. Just leave a big scratch for him to wake up to."

I focused on his chin, afraid to meet his hypnotic gaze. I'd spent too much time under his spell already.

He glanced around for potential eavesdroppers. "We can't talk here. Please, Charlie, for me. For us."

I took a breath, then gave my thoughts a voice. "I don't want to be part of your League anymore, Kade. Leave me alone."

"Nora doesn't mean anything to—"

The warning bell rang. I pushed past him.

"Charlie?"

Hugging my books to my chest, I took off, walking as fast as I could to get away from him.

The hallway was jammed with kids shuffling to class like a herd of farm animals. Crowds had never bothered me before, but now I was struggling for air. I barreled into my next class, slung my backpack against the wall, and threw myself into a chair.

I pretended that I didn't see Kade's face peering through the tiny window in the door.

♪ CHAPTER 37 ♪

ZOE SENT ME A LOOK THAT SAID IT ALL: GIVE ME A compliment, and you'll die a slow, miserable death. So I didn't say a word about the absence of mottled green and brown in her outfit. I ignored her jeans, white T-shirt, and brand-new red Converse. We sat down at the round table and ate our lunch like everyone else in the cafeteria.

As we discussed who had the worse student ID picture, I did my best to keep my eyes off Nora and Kade, who were falling all over each other at a table next to the salad bar. While I was busy trying to look somewhere else, I saw Richie emerge from the lunch line. I gestured for him to join us, but he sat alone. An island in a sea of kids. This was day three of my campaign to convince him to eat with us, and I wasn't going to give up until graduation.

When he walked by to leave the cafeteria, I called out his name. He glanced around, trained to seek out Kade.

Zoe laughed. "It's OK. We're allowed to talk now."

Richie gave her a slim smile. We started walking down the hall together.

"How have you been?" I asked him.

"It's not easy losing your best friend."

"You'll have other best friends," Zoe told him. "Better ones."

"Kade was just a dream, anyway. I woke myself up," Richie said.

Zoe didn't have a clue what he meant, but I did. Kade Harlin was as elusive as cloud formations in the sky; as soon as you figured out the picture, it changed.

At the lockers, kids rushed by us to get to class.

"Is Mr. Reid back yet?" Richie asked.

"I heard he's coming back today," Nora said, adding, "People think he's been sick."

We knew what she meant. It was eerie, the silence. No emergency assemblies. No rumors. Even the two police officers were missing in action.

We stood there, saying nothing, until Richie broke the silence. "So long, guys."

"So long," I said.

He opened his locker, took out his jacket, and walked away.

"He doesn't slouch anymore," I observed.

"That's good," Zoe said. "That's real good."

I gathered my books in my arms, too tired to put them in my backpack, and headed to my last class of the day. I was halfway down the stairwell when he stepped in front of me.

Mr. Reid.

My breath lodged in my throat.

"Hello, Charlotte."

It was good that he felt well enough to be at school. Bad that he knew my name.

"Uh, hi."

He turned to give me a close-up view of his bruised profile. "Would you meet me in my office right away?"

"Well, I have this—"

"Take a seat. I'll be there in a moment."

I nodded as he walked away.

In the office, Mrs. Roach pointed to Mr. Reid's door, then returned to a pile of forms. I walked in and sat down on the uncomfortable hard-backed chair in front of his desk. I wondered if I should take this moment to invent an alibi for prom night, but my brain felt paralyzed.

"Ah, Charlotte Brody." Mr. Reid edged past me to his desk. "I suppose you know why you're here?"

I shook my head.

He pulled out an iPhone. The iPhone. "Someone was kind enough to polish off their prints and return this to my mailbox this morning." He held it out at arm's length in front of him. "Did you know the police were able to pick up a voice when the 911 call was made from Lowell's Cemetery on the night of the prom?" His eyes shot to my face. "I think that voice was yours."

I swallowed hard, my mind shutting down. I couldn't think of a response. What should I do? What should I say?

"Why do you think it was me?" I asked after a moment.

"Because I saw you talking to Kade Harlin. He seemed angry—maybe because he believed he had a traitor in his midst."

My hands, folded in my lap, were slick with sweat. I thought of Kade's rule: *No talking in school.* He'd broken his own edict on Monday when he'd tried to convince me that I'd misinterpreted everything that had happened.

"He's a dangerous young man, Charlotte. I've been on his trail for years now because, frankly, I don't want him at Kennedy High."

He wasn't the only one. I also wanted Kade to go away, to someplace where he couldn't hurt anyone else. "He'll be gone soon," I said. "It's almost graduation."

"We both know he was behind my abduction, not to mention other unresolved incidents that have occurred at this school." Mr. Reid leaned forward, hands steepled in front of him. "I don't believe Kade and his girlfriend could cover them all."

"I'm not his girlfriend!" The denial flew out of my mouth with a force and passion that caught me off guard. I repeated it, softer, allowing the truth of it to sink in.

"The 911 call picked up more than one voice, but the clarity was poor," he said.

If the reception had been so lousy, then he couldn't really know it was me, I reasoned. All he had was a glimpse of Kade and me talking in the hall. But somehow that knowledge, though good for my situation, did nothing for my confidence.

My eyes landed on a file on Mr. Reid's desk, at least an inch thick. Kade's name was written in tight script on the upper right-hand side. Mr. Reid caught me looking. He pulled it across the desk, positioning it in front of him. "Who else was there?" he demanded.

Kade's warning at the cemetery replayed in my head: *If you tell anyone, we'll all get in trouble.*

I won't tell, I'd responded. *I could never ruin Richie, Zoe, and Nora's future.*

It was the truth. As much as I wanted to stop Kade, I couldn't pull everyone else down. Kidnapping was a felony: the difference between jail time and living our lives as normal human beings. Zoe, the poster girl for hard knocks, didn't deserve a kick to the curb from me. Then there was Richie, whose first act of courage was to ignore his best friend's murderous demands. He needed a life, not a punishment. And Nora? I didn't feel jealous if she was with Kade now. I was scared for her. I didn't want to make her life any worse than it already was.

Mr. Reid paced in front of the window, occasionally peering out at the empty running track. Then he twisted around and clamped his hands on the back of his leather chair. "Give me a list of names, and I'll do everything in my power to lighten the consequences for you. You can trust me on this."

Don't you trust me, Charlie? Kade had said.

The word crawled up my back like a cockroach. "Trust has to be earned," I said weakly.

"All I have to offer you is my word." Mr. Reid circled his chair and sat down. He waited for me to speak.

I took a slow, deep breath. "Back in January, Kade invited a group of us to join this club. He told us it was for friendship, and we believed him. He led us everywhere, like . . . like the Pied

Piper." Dad used to read me the creepy fairy tale when I was little. It was actually one of the few books he could tolerate reading more than once. "The kids in that story were beyond stupid, following a stranger for no apparent reason. I mean, the Pied Piper just had a magic pipe. But they went with him, anyway. Never to be seen again."

Mr. Reid was silent. He leaned back in his chair, thinking. "I understand, Charlotte. I truly do. Kade Harlin is a sociopath. Do you understand what that means?"

I shook my head.

"It means he lacks a conscience. He only cares about two things: winning and manipulating people to get what he wants."

Oh God. My hands trembled in my lap. I shoved them under me to stop them from shaking. How could such a simple definition fit a person who'd seemed so complex?

"Charlotte, tell me what happened, or I'm afraid there could be serious consequences for you."

Kade's words ran through my head: *Until you know otherwise, treat threats like bluffs.*

I wanted to lie, to deny every last bit of it. After all, if Mr. Reid had the evidence he needed, he wouldn't have dragged me into his office for an interrogation. But lying was what Kade would do, and I couldn't let myself think like him. Not now. Not ever.

I blinked to clear my vision. Tears spilled down the side of my nose. "I'm sorry about what happened to you, Mr. Reid."

He tapped his fingers on the file, giving away his impatience. "Do you know about Kade's past? Do you have any idea what he's done at this school? Once he gets out of here, he'll move on with his life, full speed ahead. He'll keep on hurting people."

"What did he do at Kennedy?" I asked, dreading the answer.

"The list is too long to review, but I'll give you one example," he said. "A teacher was working late when a male in a black ski mask chased her through the school. As I'm sure you can imagine, she was terrified."

"What happened to her?" I whispered.

"He shoved her down some steps and she broke her wrist. The perpetrator stole something from her, but the police don't believe that robbery was the motivation. They think he wanted to terrorize her." He picked up a pen, twirling it through his fingers like a baton. "We kept it quiet to give her time to recover from the trauma, but she'd just lost a loved one, and I'm afraid it was too much for her. She made the unfortunate, but understandable, decision to leave teaching. And now one of our PE teachers has also given notice, in part because of what happened to Fran."

Fran . . . Fran Tutti? No, not my orchestra teacher . . .

"Why would someone want to hurt a music teacher?" I asked, hoping he'd tell me that I'd made a mistake.

"Music wasn't the issue. She was a volunteer counselor who tried to address Kade's truancy problems."

I glanced down at my fingernails. I'd peeled almost all the polish off. "So you think he did it?"

Please, no. Don't let it be true.

"I know he did." The spinning pen tripped over a finger and skidded across the desk. "However, I can't prove it. My opinion of Mr. Harlin was hardly the evidence we needed in order to proceed. He's slippery, and that's the only reason he's still here." He walked over to me, placing a hand on my shoulder. "Charlotte, can you see why I need you and your friends' help?"

I prayed he'd understand what I was about to say as I raised my eyes to his. "I didn't know about your abduction before it happened. None of my friends did, either. You have no idea how much I want to tell you everything, but I can't . . . I won't."

A loud sound made us jump at the same time. I knew right away what it was, the same shrill call I'd heard the night we'd invaded the PE office. Mr. Reid's face changed from sympathetic to furious. He waited through five blasts of the fire alarm before he spoke again. "I think you and I know this is a false alarm. Probably set off by a student at this school, if I had to venture. Someone who wants you out of this office, perhaps, before his cover can be blown." Mr. Reid ran his hands down his suit, ironing out wrinkles that didn't exist. "Think on what we've discussed here, Charlotte. In the meantime, I have to investigate that alarm, since it's my job to keep the students at Kennedy safe."

He straightened his red-and-white tie and hurried out the door.

♪ CHAPTER 38 ♪

THAT AFTERNOON, I FORCED MYSELF TO LOOK AT THE notebook on my lap. Facts and dates that would be on the history final swam upstream in my head. Without warning, my anger bubbled to the surface. I lunged for the mug that was sitting on the windowsill and hurled it across the room. It hit the wall and broke in half. My hand swept across the desk, sending pens and pencils flying through the air like short-range missiles in search of a target. At last, I crumpled to the floor and buried my head in my arms.

I guess we'd all considered ourselves losers before Kade Harlin had come on the scene. Nora, the smartest of us all, had turned out to have the least common sense. As for Richie, I had no doubt that Kade believed he was still out there, bobbing aimlessly at sea. A flick of the wrist, and he could reel his friend back in. And Zoe had been too busy taking care of her mother to watch out for herself.

Then there was me. Sweet, lonely Charlotte. Another bullet point in Kade's outline. Except that I'd turned out to be a surprise ending, and if there was one thing Kade Harlin didn't like, it was surprises.

As I cleaned up from my tantrum, I promised myself that I'd never be a pawn in someone's game again. Reaching under the desk for my computer mouse, my fingers stumbled over a familiar object. Hard, cold, round. I yanked my hand back as if I'd touched a burner. I waited a moment, then scooped up the ring on a chain.

FRANCES FOREVER, 1985.

Mr. Reid's words bounced around my head: *She was a volunteer counselor who tried to address Kade's truancy problems.*

The perpetrator stole something from her.

The police didn't believe robbery was the motivation. He wanted to terrorize her.

It all made sense now. Kade had snapped the chain from Mrs. Tutti's neck and stashed the ring in his shoebox. A symbol of victory. I uncurled my fist and stared at the evidence. Kade Harlin had done this one all on his own.

Of course, if I turned Kade in, it might lead to more discoveries—discoveries that could reveal the League, but I couldn't dwell on that part. I had to focus on the one, tiny piece of proof in my hand. I owed it to Mr. Reid. I owed it to people I hadn't even met—those who would one day cross paths with Kade. He had to be stopped, no matter what.

I put the necklace down on my mouse pad, turned on the computer, and started typing.

Kade,

I'm returning the ring you gave me. I know it's Mrs.
Tutti's from the inscription. I hope you'll give it back to
her. No matter what she did to you, she deserves her
memories.

I printed it out, then taped the chain to the bottom of the
note. The ring dropped down, jumping like oil in a skillet.
Across the front of an envelope, I wrote "URGENT!" and slipped
the letter inside.

Kade wasn't the only one with a plan.

ƒ CHAPTER 39 ʅ

"AH, MISS BRODY," MR. REID SAID WHEN I WALKED INTO HIS office at lunch the next day. "Are you here to confess something?"

My stomach churned. "I've decided to help you."

I squeezed my hands together to stop them from shaking. I was risking everything—my relationship with my parents, the last vestige of friendship with Zoe and Richie, graduation. I hadn't even allowed myself to think about the two police officers, Price and Henderson, who'd spent so much time at Kennedy that they'd practically been added to the payroll. If I did, it would be even harder to go through with it.

"I have something for you." Before school, I'd fingered the wedding ring one last time, running my pinkie around its smooth interior, the inscription worn down from years of wear. The ring was a symbol of eternal union, something precious that Kade had no right to take. "It's the proof you need. Not for everything he's done. But it's enough."

Mr. Reid straightened in his chair, waiting for me to explain.

"I want Mrs. Tutti to get her husband's wedding ring back," I said. "She didn't deserve any of this. No one did."

"How'd you get . . . ?"

"Kade gave it to me after the fact. His warped idea of a present."

Mr. Reid tugged on the collar of his starched white shirt. "May I see it?"

"It's in Kade's locker. He'll stop there after lunch. I put it in an envelope with a letter. When he opens it, the ring will drop down. Anyone who's walking by will see it."

He cast his eyes to the ceiling. It was several seconds before he spoke. "I've wanted to catch Kade for a long time. I think the ring will serve that purpose. Thank you, Charlotte."

Guilt, pain, sorrow, grief—they'd hardened to stones and lodged in my heart. But here was a new feeling, rushing to the surface—gratitude.

"Thank you, Mr. Reid," I whispered.

He glanced at the clock over the door. Twenty minutes left until the bell rang, signaling the end of lunch. He rose to his feet, the way people do when they want you to leave, and unhooked his walkie-talkie from his belt.

"Mrs. Roach, please cancel my appointment with the vice president of the PTA." He switched it off and looked at me. "When I'm done, Mr. Harlin will have only me to blame."

He gave my shoulder a single pat as he passed by. I followed him to the door of the school office. We shook hands, a secret deal sealed between us.

Twelve minutes later, Mr. Reid left the office. As he turned the corner toward the hallway, I slipped into the crowd behind him.

♪ CHAPTER 40 ♫

MR. REID HID BEHIND A CEMENT POST. I DOVE BEHIND A trash can, careful to stay out of everyone's view.

And then I saw the shiny peaks of hair. Kade, at his locker, spinning the combination lock. Mr. Reid pulled the walkie-talkie free, his forehead lined in concentration.

When Kade opened the locker, the letter I'd inserted through the vents fluttered to the ground. He pulled a tube of hair gel from the upper shelf, then peered into a small mirror he'd taped to the inside door. The envelope was anchored under his left heel. He didn't even glance at it. Had he missed it? No, this was Kade Harlin. He saw everything.

Within seconds, another spike was born. At last, he bent down to pick up the envelope. The word URGENT shouted across the hall at me, but Kade ignored it, pocketing the letter.

It never occurred to me that he might not read the letter right away. If the ring didn't drop down in front of Mr. Reid, the entire plan would fail.

Kade's head swung around, scanning the crowd. I had the sinking feeling that he was looking for me. I pulled back, dizzy with fear. I could only see Mr. Reid's profile. I watched him, the walkie-talkie poised by his mouth, the veins on his hand protruding from his grip. I peered around in time to see Kade unfold my letter. I pressed a hand to my mouth, tense with expectation.

The ring on the chain dropped down, drawing circles in the air. Before I could take another breath, Mr. Reid sped across the hallway and snatched the note out of Kade's hand. He pretended to read it, jaw slack with surprise as he held up the ring. Our principal was a decent actor. Almost as good as Kade.

"That's my mother's. Give it back!" Kade demanded. Every head within thirty feet turned in his direction.

Mr. Reid lifted the ring to the light to read the inscription, then said something inaudible into his walkie-talkie. Kade raked his fingers through his hair, making an uncharacteristic mess. He took off, long steps carrying him down the hallway.

"Stop right there!" Reid called out.

Kade picked up speed, shoving a boy into the trophy case. Mr. Reid stood there, watching calmly. I didn't get it: Was he going to let Kade get away? I hugged my arms around my waist, a reminder to stay where I was. But if Kade escaped, the police would never catch him. He'd steal his uncle's BMW and be out of the state in a couple of hours, I was sure of it.

But then Mr. Jansen, the baseball coach, stepped out from behind the vending machine. The two police officers, Price and Henderson, materialized from the opposite direction. Caught between the bases, Kade had nowhere to go.

"I didn't do anything!" he shouted, shaking off Price's attempt to handcuff him. His eyes darted wildly about, searching for an exit like a squirrel caught in a trap. He spotted the nearest classroom and took off, shouldering his way toward it. If he made it inside, I knew what he'd do. He'd send a foot through the glass and tumble out the window onto the gravel sidewalk. Then he'd scramble to his feet and take off. *Gone*.

In a blur of motion, Officer Price sprinted across the room and whipped Kade's arm behind his back. Kade doubled over from the pressure Price applied to his elbow, his struggles ending in grunts of pain.

Officer Henderson snapped the cuffs onto Kade's wrists. Whispers from the crowd broke the silence, drowning out what Officer Henderson was saying to Kade. I knew the words, anyway, from watching one too many cop shows with my dad.

You have the right to remain silent. Anything you say or do can and will be held against you in a court of law . . .

I caught one last glimpse of Kade's face before he was dragged from the building. Sharp features. Angular chin. Black eyebrows knit together. Chin jutting forward in defiance. He didn't look the least bit attractive. He looked like a criminal. Kade Harlin was being removed from Kennedy High for the last time.

I allowed myself one small smile before turning to go to class. I nearly bumped into Nora, who stood beside me, so close that our shoulders practically touched. Her eyes were on the closed door as if she expected Kade to shake off the police and stroll back inside the building.

"It's over," I said, bracing myself.

Nora shifted her gaze to me, blinked the tears from her eyes, and gave a single nod. "I know."

ƒ CHAPTER 41 ʔ

AFTER MY PARENTS RANTED ABOUT MY SECRET "THING" with that "horrible boy" and recovered from shock, Dad said, "You don't need to testify at the preliminary hearing, Charlotte. They should have enough evidence to find probable cause and send him to trial."

Should have? "But what if Kade makes up a story about finding the ring somewhere?" I asked.

I could tell Dad was caught between a parental need to protect his only daughter and his legal knowledge of how to win a case. Like the good lawyer he was, the truth won out. "Yes, it would be better if you told them what he said to you," he conceded.

I didn't need to think about it anymore. "I want to testify," I said.

• • •

It was a hot June afternoon when my parents and I celebrated the court's decision to send Kade to trial. We were at Double Rainbow, and Mom was wavering between coffee crunch and rocky road when Dad's cell rang.

"Uh-huh . . . yes . . . that's what I expected . . . right. Thank you," he said into the phone.

"What?" I asked, cookie dough ice cream paused at my lips.

"That was the prosecutor," Dad said. "They've agreed to a plea bargain."

I lowered my cone. "A *what?*"

"The attorneys have proposed a sentence that they'll submit to the courts in lieu of Kade going to trial." He looked at the expression on my face, the ice cream melting down my knuckles, and said, "Ninety percent of criminal cases are settled by plea bargain, honey. It helps keep the system from getting clogged up with trials."

"Does this mean he'll get a better deal?" I asked.

"Yes, that's the trade-off."

I couldn't believe it. Where was the justice in that? "How much better?"

"The court will probably suspend some of his sentence. My guess is he'll serve one year in juvenile detention, with three years' probation."

I was stunned. "That's all?"

"He's only seventeen," Dad said. "He might straighten out his act after being locked up for a year. Maybe he'll realize there's more to life than scaring teachers."

I seriously doubted that. But I couldn't argue the point, and I couldn't tell him about all the other things Kade had done, because I hadn't told anyone—not my parents or the courts—about the League of Strays or the other plans. Just as I'd thought, Kade hadn't revealed anything more than I had, protecting all of us in the process of protecting himself.

"Serious consequences are enough to turn most people around," Dad said.

He was right about the "most people" part. But none of these people knew Kade like I did. One day, they would learn, but by then, it might be too late.

Whenever help was requested with graduation setup, or ushers needed for the musical revue, or student tutors requested to offset final-exam freak-out, I volunteered. This was my own self-inflicted community service. It was all I could do.

It was a sweltering 101 degrees on Saturday, June 16th, the day I graduated from Kennedy High. Red and white balloons floated above speakers on either side of the stage, straight in the stagnant air. Sweat trickled down my neck, snaking under my gown. I scanned the symmetrical rows for Zoe and Richie. They were lost among an ocean of graduates in identical gowns and square hats. My gaze lingered on Kade's empty chair, two rows back and four chairs over.

The class valedictorian, Emma Franklin, reached for her diploma, remembering at the last second to shake the principal's hand. Nora was wearing sunglasses, her head down. I wondered what she thought about the speech, which touted a bright future, the meaning of success, and a challenge to all of us to smile at someone on a daily basis.

In the last months of school, Nora had slipped further behind, eventually losing her grip even on salutatorian status. She looked just like the rest of us in a simple red robe.

Tiffany Miller was one of three students selected to give a graduation speech. As Kennedy High's prom princess thanked her teachers, a whistle rose from somewhere in the middle rows. Hoots followed from the back of the bleachers. Everyone stared at her, waiting for a reaction. Images of Tiffany, dress clutched to her chest, paint dripping down her arms, girls giggling into cell phones, tripped through my mind.

She tossed a disdainful look into space and continued on with her speech. "Take the good things and leave the bad behind," she concluded. "Memories are all we have to take with us."

I thought of Kade's "success" box, filled with stolen artifacts to help him remember everything he'd done. *Like getting souvenirs from the fair,* he'd said.

Tiffany finished, and the audience clapped politely. Our eyes met, and I smiled back, clapping harder. It wasn't her clichéd speech that had impressed me. It was her resilience, something I hoped to find one day.

More people joined in until the entire crowd was clapping. Tiffany grinned and bounded down the steps. She edged past Nora and plunked down into her plastic, foldout chair.

Mr. Reid ended the ceremony with some generic wishes for our future. Hats and programs were tossed into the air like a flock of birds taking flight. I climbed onto my chair to search for my parents. Mom was in the third row from the back, aiming a video camera at me. Dad was waving his arms over his head. I'd never seen him look so excited.

My viola teacher, Mr. Watson, stood beside them, primly observing the scene. I was glad he'd accepted my invitation and apology. When I'd finished the Paganini at my last lesson, he'd granted me a rare smile and said, "I suppose the vacation was good for you."

Graduates filed into the aisle, forming an endless line that slithered up the hill toward the school. I moved to the side to wait for Zoe. She practically mowed people down to catch up with me.

"Congrats, Charlotte baby," she gushed, out of breath. "Can you believe we made it?"

"Barely," came a voice behind us. Richie smiled as he wiped off the dots of sweat from his forehead with the blousy arm of his gown.

As they babbled on about graduation speeches, I spotted Nora at the top of the path, scanning the crowd. We hadn't spoken since Kade's arrest. Her gaze settled on me, her fingers curling in a tiny wave. I took a step in her direction, but she spun around and disappeared into the throng of graduates and their parents.

Richie reached into the gaping pocket of his gown and pulled out a wrinkled letter. "Guess what? I'm heading to California in three weeks."

My eyes cut to the first sentence: "The Culinary Institute is happy to inform you . . ."

Richie grinned back at me.

"Congrats, my man!" Zoe clapped him on the back. "Are you going to get one of those marshmallow hats those chef guys wear?"

"I already own three," he admitted.

"Hey, my aunt and uncle live in Sonoma," I said. I was about to suggest that I could visit him in the summer sometime, but I didn't. It may have been the polite thing to say, but it wasn't the truth. Richie and I wouldn't be seeing each other after graduation; we both knew it. As much as I cared about Richie and Zoe, I understood that Kade was the tie that bound us together, and it had almost strangled us.

"The Bay Area's beautiful," I finished.

"I hear it's cool to be gay in San Francisco," Zoe said.

Richie raised the floppy collar of his gown and struck a pose, a poor imitation of either a rock star or a vampire. I wasn't sure which. Zoe and I laughed. He was so nerdy, so completely Richie, and that, by itself, was cool.

"What are you doing this summer?" I asked Zoe.

"You're looking at the next manager-in-training at Brooks Sports. I'm going to live at home for a while, at least until my mom gets out of rehab in July."

"That's great news, Zoe," I said.

"I'm saving up for the police academy," Zoe added, squeezing her eyes shut in anticipation of our reaction. When we didn't give any, she opened them and grinned. "I can sign up when I'm twenty."

"Officer Carpenter," I said, testing it out.

"Sounds really good," Richie responded before I could.

"Who knows, maybe one day I'll get the bastard for good," she said under her breath. But we both heard her loud and clear.

"What about you?" Richie asked me.

"I'm going to State," I told them.

"What about Barrymore?" Zoe asked. "I thought you were going to call them."

"I did, but it was too late. I missed the deadline. I'm going to audition again next year. Until then, I'll keep practicing, and try out for State orchestra. Get some life experience, you know?"

"I thought the viola wasn't your thing," Richie said.

"It wasn't Kade's thing," I responded.

The three of us looked past the graduation chaos, beyond the parking lot, to the mountains that separated Glenwood from the rest of the world.

Richie and Zoe walked off, blending into the crowd of celebrating graduates. My eyes swung back to the field like a person compelled to take another look at an accident scene. Kade's chair, still empty. I knew he was out there somewhere, and all I could do was hope that, someday, I'd be able to stop looking.

ACKNOWLEDGMENTS

Thanks to my wonderful critique group and writing partners, M'Ladies of the Book: Darcey Rosenblatt, Alison Berka, and Amanda Conran. Your insightful comments over the years have made me a better writer.

A special thanks goes out to my agent, Ammi-Joan Paquette, a great writer herself, a stellar agent, and an all-around excellent person. Much gratitude goes to the team at Amulet Books, who devoted many hours behind the scenes, and to Tamar Brazis, my talented editor, for her tireless revision notes that led to the heart of my characters.

To my extended writing community and the Gango (fellow clients of the Erin Murphy Literary Agency), who are always present with advice, support, and love. Gratitude goes to my legal expert, Tyler Williams, and to the kind souls who have stepped up with valuable critiques over the years: Beryl Vaughan, Kay Allan, Trudie Scott, Laurie Huff, Osnat Oron, and Martin Hauser.

To my grandfather and fellow writer, Darrell Huff, who passed along a love of words and who once gave me a "job" that provided me with the time to launch my career and life's passion.

Immense gratitude goes out to Janice Schulman, my first editor. Her thoughts helped shape this book, and her belief in me, along with crossed fingers and toes, helped make it all happen.

Lastly, a heartfelt thanks to my family. To my daughter, Annalise, for her "plot-hole" spotting ability and valuable teen insights. Although it took cold, hard cash to get her to read it for the fifth time, I appreciate her dedication! To my youngest, Julia, a writer at heart and master of plots, who never stops thinking and sharing; and to my husband, Robert, who has worked hard and sacrificed much to buy me an invaluable stretch of time to pursue my dreams.

AUTHOR'S NOTE

In *League of Strays*, Charlotte comes to realize that revenge is a dangerous game and that those who seek it can turn into bullies themselves. Being bullied, no matter what the motivation, is never OK.

When I was growing up, bullying mostly happened at school. But today, because of unlimited access to the Internet, cyberbullying has become a serious, twenty-four-hour-a-day problem. If you or someone you know is the victim of bullying, please try to confide in a trusted adult.

Here are some places to seek help and information.

These two sites are full of resources to help deal with bullying, cyberbullying, and other teen concerns.

http://www.stopbullying.gov/
http://us.reachout.com/wecanhelpus/

The Trevor Lifeline is a 24-hour national crisis and suicide prevention lifeline for lesbian, gay, bisexual, transgender, and questioning teens.

1-866-4-U-Trevor

The GLBT National Youth Hotline provides telephone and e-mail counseling on all issues related to being a gay teen. Volunteers are in their teens and twenties.

1-800-246-PRIDE (1-800-246-7743)
youth@ GLBTNationalHelpCenter.org

This book was designed by Maria T. Middleton. The text is set in 11-point Joanna MT Regular, a typeface drawn by Eric Gill in the early 1930s and later digitized by the Monotype Foundry. The display font is Garage Gothic.

This book was printed and bound by R.R. Donnelley in Crawfordsville, Indiana. Its production was overseen by Alison Gervais.